May 11, 2024

Dear Bill, Lin, Caroline and Alex,

Hope you enjoy the read!

We love you All!

Uncle Dan
&
Aunt Deb

THE
BALLPLAYER

A Novel Based On A True Story

BY
DAVID OLIPHANT

WITH
DEBORAH A. KALMAN

the Peppertree Press
Sarasota, Florida

Registered With Writers Guild Of America East
Registration #: 1225582

This story and certain characters were, in part, inspired by actual events, persons, and organizations. Some incidents, characters, and timelines have been changed for dramatic purposes.
Some events and characters may be composites, or entirely fictitious.

Copyright © David Oliphant and Deborah A. Kalman, 2014

All rights reserved. Published by the Peppertree Press, LLC.
the Peppertree Press and associated logos are trademarks of
the Peppertree Press, LLC.

No part of this publication may be reproduced, stored in a retrieval system, transmitted in any form or by any means, electronic, mechanical, photocopying, recording, or otherwise, without prior written permission of the publisher and author/illustrator. Graphic design by Rebecca Barbier.

For information regarding permission,
call 941-922-2662 or contact us at our website:
www.peppertreepublishing.com or write to:
the Peppertree Press, LLC.
Attention: Publisher
1269 First Street, Suite 7
Sarasota, Florida 34236

ISBN: 978-1-61493-237-6
Library of Congress Number: 2014900993
Printed in the U.S.A.
Printed April 2014

Dedicated to Mom and Dad,

I'll never forget your unwaivering love and support

Preface

The story takes place in the 1950s, when baseball was at its best. Dave Roth, grew up in a tough neighborhood in the South Bronx. He was a religious Jew and a warlord of a local gang.

During a rumble with a rival gang from Spanish Harlem, Irena Rosario, his girlfriend, accidentally gets shot and killed on her way to church. Dave is considered guilty until proven innocent, and spends time in jail until his parents bail him out. He goes on to finish high school.

The New York Yankees become aware of Dave's athletic talents which leads to the Yankees signing him to a Minor League contract. He is assigned to the Class "D" Olean Yankees in upstate New York.

He has an incredibly good season and is brought up to the Major Leagues to pitch a pivotal game against the Boston Red Sox. In the meantime, the GM has a vendetta against Dave and was against the owner's decision to bring him up in the first place. He gets the dirt on Dave's past from a third party that may cause his career to be over before it begins. Does he clear his name in time to make the start?

1957, age 21
Left the Yankees and joined the Dodgers in the Macon Georgia South Atlantic League. He wore Jackie Robinson's hand-me-down uniform #42 for the entire season before the number was retired by the L.A. Dodgers.

ACKNOWLEDGEMENTS

I would like to share with you some of the wonderful people that I had the privilege of knowing during my professional baseball travels. I was truly blessed.

Eddie Lopat
My mentor—who held my hand from my junior year in high school until I signed a New York Yankees Minor League contract after graduation at the age of 17, where I was assigned to the Olean Yankees, in upstate New York, in 1953.

Hank Bauer
A great human being—I met Hank in St. Augustine, Florida at Lopat's baseball school, and then again in the Yankee Stadium, when I was called up to THE SHOW to pitch batting practice at the end of my rookie year. He was always very supportive and a very special person.

Jerry Coleman
I had the privilege of meeting Jerry Coleman, the ultimate gentleman, at baseball camp in St. Augustine, Florida. Thanks for always being so supportive.

Mickey Mantle
A great guy—always very supportive. Yes, that Mickey!

Ray and Roy Mantle
An exciting time! I roomed with Mickey's younger twin brothers, Ray and Roy Mantle, for a short time in the Cotton States League, in Monroe, Louisiana. Class acts.

Harry Hesse
The scout that signed me—thanks for being so supportive.

Del Webb
A magnificent man and co-owner of the New York Yankees. Thank you for all the courtesies you extended to me while I was in college.

Wally Lance
   I was lucky to have Wally Lance as my manager—both with the Olean Yankees and the Bristol, Virginia Yankees. He was very special.

Bobby Richardson
   A great roommate, teammate and friend—sometimes you get lucky.

Tony Kubek
   No question he was going all the way—I still remember the days in Hattiesburg, Mississippi spring training when we roomed together with 2 other guys, 4 to a room. Great memories!

Enos Slaughter
   He was a wonderful friend—thank you.

Tommy Davis
   A great roommate, great ballplayer and great friend—I was blessed to have him as my friend (my first year the Dodgers assigned me to the Hornell Dodgers in 1956, after three and a half years in the Yankees organization). Tommy, if you see this note, I still miss you.

Charlie Gilbert
   (Manager of the Hornell Dodgers) Thank you, Charlie—I will never forget how you helped me find my way—throwing the baseball my natural way. What a difference! You were very special to me.

Jackie Robinson
   A wonderful, wonderful person—I had the privilege to know him and wear his hand-me-down uniform (#42) for the entire 1957 season, in the South Atlantic League, in Macon, Georgia with the Macon Dodgers.

Curt Flood
   So proud to have been your friend. You had the courage to stand up for what you believed was right. I was honored to have worked with Curt on our book, THE WAY IT IS, and get it published by Trident Press (Simon & Schuster). I'm also proud to have played in the same league as he did in 1957.

Goldie Holt
(Manager of the Macon Dodgers, 1957) A special person and always encouraging—I was proud to have known you and played for you.

Roy "Campy" Campanella
A gem—so sad that your career was cut short by that terrible accident. Thank you for supporting my Leukemia Society efforts to raise money to help find a cure. Campy, we won!

Tommy Lasorda
True blue. Probably the most loved Dodger that ever lived and played the game—and a terrific person. Thanks, Tommy, for your support and the shirt!

Danny Ozark
A great manager—that I held in high esteem.

Sandy Koufax, Carl Furillo, Carl Erskine
I made the first cut in Vero Beach, Florida spring training and went with the team to play in the Grapefruit League in Miami, Florida where it was my honor and privilege to have shared a 2-bedroom suite at the McAllister Hotel with 3 baseball icons.

Buzzy Bavasi
A special thanks—for always being so supportive.

Al Campanis
Thank you, Al—I will never forget the confidence you had in me to bring me over from the New York Yankees to the Brooklyn Dodgers.

Ralph Branca
Always terrific—it's sad he is remembered for the wrong thing. You were a wonderful pitcher and a great person Thank you for your support.

Joe Pignatano
A special human being and terrific player—thank you for your support. I loved babysitting your kids for you and your wife.

Carl Spooner
Absolutely wonderful—thank you for all the lessons in life!

Branch Rickey
Although I never met you—I will always remember your heroism. You are special in baseball history.

Marvin Miller
How blessed the Players' Association was—having you as its president. You are greatly missed.

Bill Virdon
A memorable time—thank you for the opportunity to work at your baseball camp in Tampa, Florida.

Coach Nick Chiketti
Thank you. I'll never forget how supportive you were. You are a credit to the teaching profession and a fine person.

Harold Sternberg
Thank you for your patience and support. You are a wonderful memory in my life.

Joe Montalvo
My Bronx brother, we came close. Your friendship will never be forgotten. Those were wonderful years in the Minor Leagues—even though we played against each other.

Dom Montalbano
Everyone should be blessed with a coach like you. I was honored to play baseball and basketball for you at Morris High School. You will always be very special to me.

Jack Vallely
My college mentor. Just a special person in my life that I'm indebted to for discovering me at Bill Virdon's baseball school where I was an instructor. You got me a full baseball and basketball scholarship to Curry College. It was a major turning point in my life. Thank you, Jack!

Charles "Chuck" Blankfort
A great friend and partner. I'll never forget you.

Table of Contents

ACKNOWLEDGEMENTS 1
SPORTS TIMELINE 7
SUMMARY 9

- CHAPTER 1: The Rumble 11
- CHAPTER 2: The Front Office 18
- CHAPTER 3: The Olean Yankees 23
- CHAPTER 4: The Dirt On Dave Roth 35
- CHAPTER 5: The Night Before 40
- CHAPTER 6: The Championship Game 46
- CHAPTER 7: Playing With The Big Boys 55
- CHAPTER 8: Victory Night 61
- CHAPTER 9: Home, Sweet Home 70
- CHAPTER 10: Back In The Bronx 75
- CHAPTER 11: Trouble Brewing 85
- CHAPTER 12: Sandy Abrams 91
- CHAPTER 13: The Yankee Stadium 100
- CHAPTER 14: Back In The Neighborhood 108
- CHAPTER 15: Bad Press 115
- CHAPTER 16: Just A Hunch 123
- CHAPTER 17: The Last Supper 130
- CHAPTER 18: The Big League Bigot 139
- CHAPTER 19: Debbie The Detective 148
- CHAPTER 20: The Troubled Outcast 154
- CHAPTER 21: The Windup 160
- CHAPTER 22: Clearing The Air 171
- CHAPTER 23: Straight To The Top 181
- CHAPTER 24: The Big Game – The Show 187
- CHAPTER 25: Top Of The Ninth 193
- CHAPTER 26: A Happy Ending 199

McAllister Hotel Lobby In Miami, FL

The hotel where the LA Dodgers stayed during The Grapefruit League. What an experience!

The Mayor of Macon, Georgia, B.F. Merritt, Jr. giving Dave a check to buy an Israeli Bond, 1957.

SPORTS TIMELINE

1948: **P.S. 52 Junior High School, Bronx New York –**
Varsity Basketball and Softball

1949-1953: Morris High School, Bronx, New York –
Varsity Baseball, Basketball, Soccer, Bowling

1953: **Olean Yankees, Olean, New York – New York Yankees Minor League Team:** Pennsylvania-Ontario-New York (PONY) League, Class D

1953: **Brought up to the New York Yankees in September to pitch batting practice.**

1954: **New York Yankees, St. Joseph, Missouri –**
American Association, Minor League, Class A

1954: **New York Yankees, Bristol, Virginia –**
Appalachian League, Minor League, Class D

1955: **Invited to Spring Training with the New York Yankees, St. Petersburg, Florida:** Brought up to New York Yankees (at the end of our Minor League season), Bronx, New York, to work out with the Yankees and pitch batting practice.

1955: **New York Yankees, Binghamton, New York – Eastern League,** Minor League, Class A

1955: **New York Yankees, Monroe, Louisiana – Cotton States League,** Minor League, Class C

1955: **New York Yankees, Pine Bluff, Arkansas –**
Cotton States League, Minor League, Class C

1955: **New York Yankees, Meridian, Mississippi –**
Cotton States League, Minor League, Class C

1956: **Brooklyn Dodgers, Hornell, New York** – Brooklyn Dodgers Minor League Team: Pennsylvania-Ontario-New York (PONY) League, Class D

1957: **Invited to Spring Training with the Brooklyn Dodgers,** Vero Beach, Florida, and made the first cut.

1957: **Brooklyn Dodgers (last year as Brooklyn Dodgers), Macon, Georgia** – South Atlantic League, Minor League, Class A. (NOTE: See attached picture of author, who wore the hand-me-down uniform of Jackie Robinson for the entire season.)

1958: **Invited to Spring Training with the Los Angeles Dodgers (first year as Los Angeles Dodgers),** Vero Beach, Florida

1958: **Los Angeles Dodgers, Macon, Georgia** – Minor League, Class A

SUMMARY

In 1959, I graduated from Curry College, in Milton, Massachusetts, where I played baseball and basketball on a full scholarship. I was proudly voted into their Hall of Fame in both sports.

- In 1960, I accepted a teaching position in Abington, Massachusetts, as a junior high school teacher and the head baseball coach of the high school team – winning the district championship.

- In 1967, while living in Westport, Connecticut, I became active – and remained so for over 20 years, as a player and a coach – in all sports – from slow-pitch softball leagues (as a player) to Little League to Babe Ruth and finally to American Legion (coaching and managing). This was an incredible experience that I loved.

- My dream has always been to be a third base coach or bench coach for a Major League team, especially for the Yankees. I love working with young baseball players and helping them gain confidence and develop their skills. Great memories!

Hornell Dodgers, 1956
PONY League

Pine Bluff, Arkansas, "Cotton States League"
Class "C", 1955. New York Yankees affiliate.

CHAPTER 1

The Rumble

"Someday, Dave," she murmured, "you're going to be a star."

Growing up in the South Bronx as the 1940s ended and the 1950s began, there were two things I loved, Irena Rosario and baseball.

Irena held my hand, and for a second I got lost in her beautiful eyes, the color of deep, dark chocolate. "Just promise me that you won't go tonight," she said.

"There's nothing to worry about," I said.

"Alejandro is very angry," she said. "And when my cousin is angry, he is uncontrollable. He says you and the other Wildcats have crossed the line."

I shook my head. "When they cross the bridge from East Harlem, they're on our turf."

Alejandro was the warlord of the Rockets, the major gang of Spanish Harlem and long-time rivals of the Bronx Wildcats. As the Wildcats warlord, I was supposed to be Alejandro's sworn enemy. But ever since meeting Irena a few months earlier, it was hard for me to hate him.

"I have a bad feeling about tonight, Dave," she said, her voice barely above a whisper.

Her parents also weren't crazy about her going steady with a Jew, and my parents weren't crazy about me going out with a Catholic Puerto Rican.

"This will be just like all the other rumbles. A few bloody noses, a few cracked knuckles. Nothing to lose any sleep over," I told her.

"Just promise me you'll be careful," Irena said. She took my face in her hands and said, "I care about you, Dave Roth."

"I care about you, too," I said, kissing her lightly on the cheek.

When I wasn't on the streets with the Wildcats, I was playing ball. Thanks to a great fastball and a mean curveball, along with a batting average that wasn't too shabby, I earned a reputation as one of the best high school ballplayers in all of New York City. The previous summer, in 1951, my teammate Hank Alier, the scrappy second baseman on the Morris High School baseball team, asked me, "Dave, how 'bout playing on our Police Athletic League baseball team this summer? The season starts as soon as school's out."

"What's it all about?" I asked, sounding doubtful.

He said, "It's a competitive league for fourteen- to eighteen-year olds. Our team's called the Colonials. It's a twenty-four-game schedule—so we play three times a week and finish up by the end of August. We've got uniforms, umpires, and a really nice field. We play at Babe Ruth., right across from Yankee Stadium." "Wow, that's a great field," I said.

"What does it cost?" I asked him.

"Nothing. We collect donations. My dad gets a lot from his company. He's our manager, too. He was at our Morris High game last week and saw you pitch. C'mon—play for us!"

"Okay, I'm in!"

So I played with the Colonials. My team ended up in first place in the PAL league—we won a lot of trophies. So, that summer turned out to be a positive turning point in my life.

The Rumble

It also turned out to be one hell of a good time.

There was always bad blood between the Wildcats and the Rockets. Most of the Wildcats were pretty good kids. Our gang was like a family—we stuck together, didn't get into a whole lot of trouble, and had each other's backs. The Rockets, on the other hand, had a very bad reputation. They were dangerous, and most of them had police records.

We stayed in our own territories—the Rockets in Spanish Harlem and the Wildcats in the South Bronx—for years, but now Alejandro had crossed a line. He had laid claim to St. Mary's Park in the South Bronx, which had been a part of Wildcat and Irish Dukes territory for as long as anyone could remember.

Ever since I'd become the warlord, I tried to channel my boys' energies into competitive sports rather than fighting. Yet I knew it in my blood this wasn't something that could be settled with a game of stickball. Alejandro meant business.

I loved Irena, I loved stickball and I loved baseball, but I couldn't turn my back on my boys. When I kissed her goodbye that afternoon on "tar beach"—the roof of her apartment building—I tried to make her feel at ease, but it didn't work.

It was April 29, 1952. We didn't know it at the time, but all of our lives were about to change drastically.

That night the Wildcats met up in the P.S. 62 schoolyard. As the warlord, I gave a rally speech.

"The Rockets have screwed with us long enough," I said. "It's time we send them back to where they came from. The South Bronx is our turf."

I looked around at my boys. They were carrying rocks and baseball bats, except Big Joe, one of the older gang members who had always

The Ballplayer

been jealous that I was warlord instead of him, he pulled out a homemade zip gun.

"I'll show those spics who's boss," he said.

Big Joe was trouble. He was in and out of juvie for the last few years and dropped out of school. His Dad was a mean drunk who kicked Big Joe's ass more than once.

"Leave the gun at home, Big Joe," I said, giving him a stern look.

"You afraid, Davey?" he said, testing me.

"I'm not afraid." I responded angrily. "I'm just not stupid."

"If we don't want them to mess with us," he replied, ignoring my insult, probably not realizing he was being insulted, he said, "we gotta lay down the law."

The other Wildcats looked at me. They were waiting for me to make the final call.

I shook my head. "You know the rules, guys. No guns."

"And what if the Rockets bring blades?" piped up one of the younger Wildcats.

"They won't," I said. "I'll hold Alejandro to his word."

"Whatever you say," Big Joe grunted, backing down. But his eyes flashed a warning. "You're the boss, Davey. If something goes wrong, it's on your hands."

I tried to shake off what Big Joe said, but it stuck in my head. He was right and I knew it.

We were like coiled springs of tightly wound metal—the slightest thing would set us off.

When we got to St. Mary's, the Rockets were waiting. Alejandro stepped out of the shadows to meet me.

"Today, you'll all pay," he said, with no hesitation and anger. "And you—" Alejandro pointed directly at me and raised his voice so everyone could hear. "You'll pay for seducing my cousin. Irena deserves better than a dirty kike."

The minute he said that, total chaos erupted. The gangs flew at each other, hitting one another with bats, pipes and fists. There were over a hundred of us in all, everyone fueled by rage.

In the heat of the moment, I forgot everything I'd promised Irena.

The Rumble

I forgot that this wasn't who I wanted to be, that I loved baseball and dreamed of a future beyond gang fights. I forgot who I was. I forgot it all. Instead, I unleashed a full force of fury at Alejandro and his gang. I was a one-man wrecking machine.

It didn't take me long to realize that the Rockets had broken their promise. They brought knives.

It was bloody—broken noses, cut arms. I felt Alejandro's blade slide into my back.

I fell to the ground, just in time to hear a woman's scream.

"DAVID!"

I looked up, and there she was. It was Irena, running toward me from across the park in a long flowing white dress. I thought I must be dreaming.

"DAVID!" she screamed again.

Then I knew. She was real, and she was there. Irena was in the park, in the middle of an out-of-control rumble.

Out of the corner of my eye, I saw Alejandro turn toward her in surprise.

"Irena!" He yelled something in Spanish. "What are you doing here? Go home, primita! Go home, now!"

Suddenly, I heard a different sound, like a baseball being ripped apart at the seams, like the sound of a home run. But it wasn't a baseball. It was the sound of a handgun. I watched as Irena stumbled, clutched her chest, and fell to the ground.

And then I realized – she'd been shot.

Madness erupted all around us. I started crawling across the grass, trying to get to her.

"Irena!" I called out, "Irena, get up! Go home!"

Then I heard sirens . . . the cops.

I no longer cared about anything. I let the moment carry me away, and gave in to the fury running through my veins. I watched the Rockets scatter, tucking their knives into their jeans and pockets as they ran from the police. I reached around for anything I could get my hands on. I found dozens of rocks that had been thrown or dropped. I began throwing them as hard as I could. I just kept throwing rocks, with every ounce of strength I could muster, hitting the remaining Rockets with frightening precision.

Until I felt a strong hand on my arm.

"Give it up," a deep voice said. "Drop it. We're taking you in."

I let go of the rock I was holding as I felt myself being picked up under the arms and lifted from the ground. Pain rushed through my left shoulder, but I kept struggling. I had to get to Irena.

Through the blur, I thought I saw her being lifted onto a stretcher by a group of men in uniform. A big red stain was visible on her white dress.

"Irena!" I called out again.

It was too late. The officers were dragging me away.

I sat in the squad car, my forehead pressed against the glass, and watched the medics. They were calm and controlled. I wanted to scream at them to do something—to save her. She was still and not moving.

"Hey kid," said the officer in the front seat.

I could barely find the energy to reply.

"Sir?" I said.

"You're in a lot of trouble." He said.

I nodded, still watching Irena through the window.

I let out a sharp cry.

"What the—" The officer touched my shoulder and pulled back his hand. It was covered in blood. "You've been stabbed! Why didn't you say something?"

"I wasn't sure..." My voice drifted off as the colors around me began to swim. I was being walked out of the squad car by the officer to the emergency room door at Lincoln Hospital. I tried to walk toward Irena, whose white dress was now red.

My knees buckled underneath me as my legs gave out. "Irena!" I called out, one last time. I staggered forward. A doctor was by my side immediately, examining my wound, asking me questions. He told me I'd lost a lot of blood and asked if I could tell him exactly what happened. I couldn't answer. I was woozy and sick to my stomach.

"Is she okay?" I said.

The doctor looked at me and said, "I'm sorry." He shook his head. "The Spanish girl outside, she's gone."

The last thing I remember is a firm hand on my shoulder. Then everything went black as I sank like a dead weight onto the floor.

CHAPTER 2

The Front Office

"I don't like it, Casey." "Fletch", GM of the New York Yankees, yelled out, "I don't like that one bit."

"I don't like it either, Fletch. But we don't have much of a choice." Casey, the Yankee manager said softly.

Howie McPherson, called "Mac", owner of the Yankees, was easily bullied by his GM Fletch. Mac is a real estate genius who had bought the team as a profitable hobby.

Mac loved beautiful women, cafe society, seeing his name in the headlines, and backslapping with the guys at Toots Shor's, Club 21, and the other top watering holes in Manhattan. He grew up a baseball fan, worshipping the Yankees of the 1920s and 1930s. He turned his family's small fortune in real estate into an empire. When the opportunity to buy the Yankees became available, he jumped all over it. He was a delegator in his real estate businesses and took the same approach with his baseball team. Find someone great and let him do things their way. Fletch took advantage of Mac's hands-off approach, he considered it a sign of weakness.

"Lookie here, guys," Mac said. "You know the game. I know the numbers. If what you're telling me is true, I see a big opportunity to get us some much-needed positive publicity. All this business about the Yankees being slow to sign a Negro has got to be hurting us at the gate."

"Publicity?" Fletch frowned. "How do you figure?"

"Because if you do what we're suggesting," Mac said, rubbing his palms together, "you're going to turn a nobody into an instant star. And if there's one thing that the American public loves, it's a rags-to-riches story."

THE FRONT OFFICE

"I'll tell you one thing the American public hates," Fletch began, with an arrogant tone... 'Is some bush leaguer that nobody's ever heard of causes us to lose a potential pennant clinching game against the Red Sox."

That shut Mac up, and Casey played it safe and stayed quiet.

In 1932, Martin Fletcher, had been hired by the Yankees to create a farm system based on the successful model he pioneered with the St. Louis Cardinals. He used the Minor Leagues as a training ground for the Major Leagues. It was also a good way to develop popular support for the game of baseball in cities too small for a Major League team. Minor League teams were a major form of entertainment in small town America.

Fletch, as he was called, was in his mid-forties, and uncommonly ambitious. By 1938, he'd created a dozen Minor League teams in twelve different leagues that consistently turned out outstanding players. Their Minor League system helped the Bronx Bombers to win five straight pennants. In the late 1940s, Fletch convinced Mac to name him the GM of the Yankees.

"I want to win our sixth consecutive pennant," Fletch said plainly, "but I haven't seen or heard about any real talent in the Minor Leagues this year."

"That's not what I heard, Fletch," Mac said as he turned to Casey. "Tell us what you know."

Casey spoke slowly, choosing his words with great care. The double talk routine was something he reserved for the press. "We've got some damn good players in our Minor League system. A couple of guys in particular stand out."

Mac shook his head. "Look, Fletch, facts are facts. Our team is in a dogfight with Cleveland. The Tribe's got the blade right to our necks, and it's gonna be a real close race."

Fletch said "A small lead and injured pitchers. Not a winning combination in my book."

He gave Casey a hard look. "What's the word on Raschi and Reynolds?"

"It don't look good," Casey admitted. "The trainer says Vic should rest his arm for a couple of weeks, and Allie's under strict orders to stay in bed."

"And Lopat?" Fletch asked.

Casey answered, "We've overworked him as it is, Fletch. If Cleveland keeps playing the way they have been, we're going to need Eddie big time. Pitch him too much now, and we could burn him out for the stretch when we really need him."

"So you're telling me we've got no choice but to bring up a Minor Leaguer for a spot start in Yankee Stadium? We're talking about bringing up a kid from a Class "D" Minor League team...to face the Red Sox and Ted Williams...while we're in the race for the American League pennant? Am I hearing this right?" Fletch asked.

Casey answered...If Cleveland loses one game, and we beat the Red Sox, the pennant is ours—It's a clinch!"

"It's the only choice we have, guys," Casey said firmly.

Mac jumped back into the conversation.

"Don't you see the opportunity here, guys?" he asked, as his excitement grew. "We take a kid from the Minor Leauges, someone with a great arm who's really hungry for this shot, and give it to him. It's dynamite! We bring him up, let him pitch, and watch the crowds go wild. It's history in the making—a homegrown star makes it to The Show. Every kid in that stadium is gonna to sit there and think, 'Hey, that could be me!' It'll do wonders for ticket sales and our image."

"We've had good luck with the kids we've brought up so far," Casey admitted. "You've done a great job Fletch, putting those bush league teams together. And I hear the scouts are pretty damn impressed with what they've seen this year from some of our young pitchers."

Fletch turned in his chair. "What exactly have they seen?"

"Well," Casey stammered, "they've seen this particular pitcher throw as much as a 100-mile-an-hour fastball without any arm strain and pinpoint control. They saw the same kid strike out twenty – in one game. Now it may be "D" ball, but that's damn good pitchin' anywhere in my book."

Mac raised his eyebrows. "Twenty K's in one game, Casey? Now we're talking, boys, now we're talking! Who's the player?"

THE FRONT OFFICE

Casey took a deep breath. "Kid's name is Dave Roth."

"Roth?" Fletch and Mac said together.

"That's the guy," Casey said firmly.

Fletch's eyes darkened. "Never heard of him."

"The kid's barely eighteen and he's already a Minor League legend." Casey began to speak more quickly, hardly able to contain his excitement. "I'll tell you what I know. Roth was considered the best high school ballplayer in all of New York City. He graduated from Morris High School in the South Bronx this past May. People say he's the second coming of Hank Greenberg, who went to Monroe—Morris's arch rival." Casey paused. "He's also a Jew boy."

"A Jew, huh?" Fletch said, his voice flat.

"Now wait a minute," Mac said, slowly putting the pieces together. "We haven't had a good Jewish ballplayer since Jimmy Reese in the 1920s?'

"We also had that guy Karpel in '46." Fletch said ignoring Mac's attempt to convince him. "And he was no Babe Ruthowitz."

"I don't care what he is" Casey said. "If he can throw 100-miles-an-hour and strikes, he's my boy."

Mac slapped his knees, his exuberance startling the others. "This is it! This is it! Don't you see? This is exactly what we need, a homegrown Jewish ballplayer, bringing Roth up will help us keep faith with our Jewish fans. And maybe take some of the heat off us for not signing a Negro."

"Plus, he's a damn good ballplayer," Casey added.

Both men looked at Fletch, whose face was unreadable. He was known for his stoicism and the fact that no one ever knew what he was thinking. Now was no exception.

"What do you think, Fletch?" Mac asked. He was the owner, and gave the final word to his GM. Fletch said, "Sounds like this is the way to solve all our problems—bring in a player with all the marks of a champion, and get some goodwill with our Jewish fans at the same time."

Fletch exhaled a long, agonizingly slow puff of smoke from his Cuban. He tapped it into the crystal ash tray on his desk.

"Seems to me it's pretty clear what we should do," Mac said, brushing the ash off his suit. He cleared his throat. "But we need you to be on board."

In an attempt to follow Mac's lead, Casey cleared his throat and stood up.

"Where the hell do you think you're going, Casey?" Fletch barked.

In a flash, Casey sat back down. He might have been one of the most colorful and celebrated managers in baseball history, but in the Yankees organization, and especially in the estimation of the GM, he was just another employee.

"We're far from done here, gentlemen," Fletch said, his voice dripping with sarcasm.

"I'll be damned if I sign on before I get more information."

"Get me some more options," Fletch said, banging his fists on the desk. "You get me a list of potential starters by tomorrow night. Understand? And then you get me the dirt on this Roth guy. I want to know who he is, how he plays. I want to know everything about him, from the way he ties his shoes to the way he likes his eggs. I want his mother's maiden name and his high school record. Got it? Understand? Then, and only then, will I make my decision. Have I made myself clear, gentlemen?"

Mac and Casey nodded their heads like scolded schoolchildren.

"Very good," Fletch said, crushing the life from his cigar. "We'll meet in my office tomorrow night, after the game. Meeting adjourned."

CHAPTER 3

The Olean Yankees

It had been nearly eighteen months since the rumble at St. Mary's Park. The rumble with the Rockets had cost me a lot more than a night in the hospital and some stitches in my left shoulder —it had cost me my love, Irena.

The police couldn't find the murder weapon, even though I had a pretty good idea who had it and shot Irena. The image of Big Joe O'Neill with his homemade zip gun was forever etched in my mind. He didn't come forward to confess his part in Irena's death, and I wasn't going to rat out one of my own.

So I took the blame. That's what a warlord does. I spent three weeks in the slammer—three long, hot weeks sleeping on the dirty, rat-infested floor and eating slop that even a pig would have refused. Finally, my Dad was able to get several loans and put together enough money to secure a lawyer who presented a case for my release, at least until more evidence was gathered and the real killer came forward.

"Dave Roth is innocent," my attorney declared, but there was still doubt.

I knew there was no blood on my hands, and my father and mother knew it too. But as for the rest of the world, how could they be sure? Dave Roth was a former warlord, a gang leader in the South Bronx. "A good kid," people said, "but he went down the wrong path."

Remarkably, I even made it back to Morris for my senior year, in September, 1952. I got out of jail just a few days before classes started. I went back to high school as a social outcast—nobody wanted to hang with me, the guy who spent part of the summer in jail and was charged with killing his girlfriend, and was **guilty until proven innocent!**

The Ballplayer

One day that fall, I got a call from Lieutenant Fabrizi, the arresting officer in my case.

"Got a minute, Dave?" He asked.

I said, "Officer, I've been advised not to talk to anyone without my lawyer present."

Fabrizi chuckled. "I'm not calling to talk about your case, Dave. I'm calling to talk about your arm."

"My arm?" I repeated, touching my shoulder carefully. Despite a brief infection during the time I spent in jail, the knife wound had healed pretty well. "It's okay, Officer. Thanks for your concern."

"Glad to hear it, Dave. Glad to hear it. That's why I'm calling."

"You've got my attention," I said, waiting for him to continue.

"I saw you throwing those rocks." He paused.

"I gotta say...where did you ever learn to throw like that?"

This caught me totally off guard.

He let out a low whistle. "You've got quite an arm. Didn't I also see you playing baseball in the PAL League?"

"I...I did play," I stammered, unable to reconcile the idea that I was under arrest for a role in a gang fight murder and yet somehow I'm talking about baseball with a cop. I answered,

"Last summer I pitched for the Colonials."

"No kidding?" he said. "So, that's where I saw you." "Yeah, well anyway, I do private security at the Yankee Stadium when I'm not on duty. I also bird dog for them. I think they'd like to see what you've got."

The words still weren't making sense to me. The Yankees? Baseball?

"Well, guess what, Dave? You got yourself a tryout at Yankee Stadium with Harry Hesse, the head New York State Yankee scout. Can you be there tomorrow morning at eight?"

My voice disappeared. Hesse was legendary, the scout whose normal territory was upstate New York who would come all the way to the Bronx, to see me pitch. I'd be throwing in front of a guy who could make my career and get me off the streets.

"Yes!" I managed to stammer. "Yes, sir! Thank you."

"Good. They're expecting you."

I could almost see Lieutenant Fabrizi's smile as he hung up the phone.

And that's how it began. On Saturday, September 14, 1952, I threw off the mound in what I thought was an otherwise empty Yankee Stadium for an audience of one--Harry Hesse. He stood along the first base line, arms crossed, saying nothing, watching me throw to Charlie Silvera, the third-string catcher for the Yankees.

Hesse didn't say anything the whole time I threw. Good thing, because my first three pitches went over Silvera's head. I had a slight case of nerves. I mean, it's the Yankee Stadium, for Pete's sake. Silvera saw that I was tense and he flipped up his mask, came out to me, handed me the ball, and said, "It'll never be this easy again, kid. Usually you got a guy with a bat standing up there. Relax and show us what you got."

I was so grateful to Silvera for his kindness. I settled down and threw strikes--fastballs, a change, and a slider. I had a wicked slider and it was working for me that day. Hesse was noticeably impressed with what he saw.

Suddenly, another player stepped out of the shadows. It was Eddie Lopat, a starting pitcher for the New York Yankees.

I couldn't believe it. Lopat was watching me pitch. All I could say was, thank God I didn't known he was there. If I'd known, I would have been even more nervous.

Lopat must have liked what he saw, too, because he walked over to me, extended his hand, and said, "Nice throwing, kid."

"Th-thank you, Mr. Lopat," I stammered. He seemed even taller and more imposing in person than in the newsreels.

Mr. Lopat actually told me to come back the following Saturday, and all the Saturdays after that. Before I knew what was happening, he was working with me one-on-one whenever the Yankees were in town, as fall, 1952 flew by.

For reasons I'll never know, Mr. Lopat took a special interest in me. He spent a lot of time transforming me into a pitcher as opposed to merely a hard thrower.

"You've really got something special, Dave," Lopat said to me after watching one of my hundred mile an hour fastballs.

"Thanks," I responded, trying not to stammer.

"I think you're ready for the next drill."

"What's that, sir?"

"The strings."

One of his drills for helping pitchers develop pinpoint control was throwing to a catcher with "strings." In this setup, there were two wooden stands in front of home plate and the catcher— each about the height of the average player, was five-foot-nine. Two strings were dropped vertically from shoulder to knees, over home plate. This created a box made of strings, and anything inside that box was the strike zone.

Throwing inside the strings was the objective, and as my skills improved, Mr. Lopat pulled the strings closer together, making the box smaller and smaller. The goal was to end up with a six-inch by six-inch square string box that could be moved anywhere within the strike zone. This was called "painting the plate".

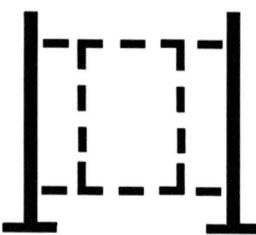

Eddie Lopat's Strings

Mr. Lopat taught me how to throw a curveball that dropped off a table and how to change up my fastball and curveball, which is a slow pitch. I showed my coach at Morris, Dom Montalbano, who I considered a great friend, what I learned. Even though I was good before, now I was a force to be reckoned with. I had four new pitches and excellent control.

Mr. Lopat told me I was a shoe-in to be signed.

One night in the spring, Mr. Lopat and Mr. Hesse showed up unexpectedly at our apartment door while we were having dinner. My folks and I had huge grins of surprise on our faces.

"Ready to play for the Yankees?" Lopat said. He was holding a Yankee cap in his hands. He put it on my head and gave me an affectionate punch in the arm." My parents were in a state of shock as I introduced them.

And that's how it came to pass that in April, 1953, a month before my high school graduation, I signed a contract with the New York Yankees and was assigned to the Olean Yankees Minor League team in upstate New York. The day after graduation, I set out for Olean, New York.

The Olean Yankees were a Minor League "class-D" team, the lowest level of professional baseball. It was also a part of the Pennsylvania/Ontario/New York League, affectionately called the PONY League. The team was already nearly two months into their season when I arrived.

I was seventeen-years-old, soon to be eighteen. I weighed about a hundred and ninety pounds, stood around six-foot-two—I was a lean, strong, and very muscular, right-handed pitcher, a good hitter and outfielder, from the South Bronx. I also had a criminal record. I spent three weeks in jail, wrongfully accused in the murder of Irena Rosario, the girl that was the love of my life.

Olean, a small town in upstate New York, was a great place to play baseball.

Before our last season game, while I was in the dugout watching the tail end of batting practice, Skip, our manager, tapped me on the shoulder.

"Need to see you in Shultzy's office before the game tonight," he said. Shultzy was our GM. He's the guy you saw when the team was giving you your release.

"Sure," I said, wondering what was up. Usually nothing good. But I was pitching good, so what could they be thinking?

"Do I need to bring anything?" I asked, nervously.

"Just yourself."

Skip, whose name was Wally Lance, a stand-up guy and also our playing manager, if he knew something, he would tell me what was up.

The more I thought about it, the more I began to worry. Maybe my past was finally catching up to me. Maybe all the happiness and triumph I experienced over the last few months, pitching well and swinging a hot bat, too, was coming to an end.

My palms were sweaty as we made our way to Shultz's tiny office. He was in his late thirties but looked older—about five-foot-nine and balding. Shultzy, as we called him, always looked like he meant business.

There were a dozen voices saying different things in my head. Surely they weren't going to release me. I was having a storybook season. I never played better. When all the new players had arrived in June, me included, the Olean Yankees were in dead last place and the Jamestown Tigers were in first. By the time the end of the season rolled around we were just one game away from clinching a tie for first place. If we beat Corning tonight, we would have a one-game playoff for the PONY League championship with the Jamestown Tigers.

I was a pivotal player in all the games I started, but even I had to admit that I was like a man without a country. I did a little of everything—starting pitcher, relieving, long relief, closer, playing the outfield, first base or pinch-hitting in between starts. Whatever I was asked to do, I did well, but maybe that didn't cut the mustard with the Yankees front office.

Skip and Shultzy sat side by side. I was eager to get the whole thing over and done with. I gave them my best. If that wasn't good enough for the Yankee organization, then screw 'em.

"You alright, Dave?" Shultz asked. He motioned me to a chair, and I sank into it.

"I'm doin' okay, sir."

"You sick?" He asked.

"No."

"Then what's wrong?" Skip asked.

I looked at Shultzy nervously before deciding to get it all out of my system. If they called me in to release me, I decided to quit first. I still had my pride. "Lay it on me," I told him. "I'm packed, ready to catch the next bus back to the Bronx. Just give me my ticket."

There was dead silence. Finally, Shultzy asked, "What the hell are you talking about?" staring at me like I was nuts.

I looked at him for a moment. "Aren't you going to tell me I've been released?" I answered.

"Are you crazy?" he blurted out, his voice growing louder. "You're the backbone of our pitching staff! That's what we wanted to talk to you about."

"Look, Dave," Skip said, taking over. "We can win the championship, and it'll be great for everyone. Maybe Shultzy and me will even get out of Class "D". Here's the deal—we want to start you in left field today and then you can pitch in the championship game, if we win today."

Schultzy glared for a moment at Skip, possibly for violating the baseball taboo that said you never looked ahead past the current game.

"We want you in left field," Schultzy said, turning to me, "because we need your bat in the lineup. If Thompson starts to fade, we'll bring you in to finish 'em off. It's a little unorthodox but it's definitely within the rules. That way, we can still have you ready to pitch the playoff game."

"Sure!" I said, relieved they weren't releasing me. It's funny how the mind plays tricks. I wasn't going anywhere except left field. I said, "Let's go kick some Corning butt!"

The ballpark was packed with fans, everyone cheering at the top of their lungs. In Olean, we were heroes.

I was antsy, trying to stay cool. The vote of confidence from Shultzy and Skip meant a lot to me. Maybe things would be all right after all.

When the game with Corning started, we jumped out to an early lead. Corning went down, one two three in the top of the first--our pitcher, Art Thompson was on fire. I led off our half of the first with a walk and Bobby and Candle hit back-to-back doubles. Bobby and Candle were my roommates, both great guys and damn good ballplayers. Candle's real name was Roman Vilchez, but we had quickly nicknamed him "Candle" because he was long and lanky like a candlestick. By the time Art got to pitch the top of the second, we were up 4–0.

But Art got a little careless with that big lead. Going into the bottom of the seventh, we were leading 7–5, a little too close for comfort. You could even feel the tension in the crowd when they got up for the seventh inning stretch.

Skip motioned to Jorge, one of the younger pitchers who hadn't played much all season.

"Go warm up," he said. Jorge look shellshocked, but he immediately followed Skip's instructions.

Art was tiring fast. We needed some more runs. I was leading off the bottom of the seventh and hoped I could get something going. Concentrate, I told myself, and it seemed to work. BANG—a high fly to right, which bounced over the outfielder's head and into the seats for a ground rule double.

After that, Bobby grounded out to the second baseman and moved me to third. Candle hit a rocket past the first baseman, I scored, and he was held at first. Stoney hit into a double play. Score: 8–5.

We had the lead, but Corning wasn't giving up. They weren't laying down for anyone. They weren't in the hunt for the playoffs, they were playing spoiler and they kept on coming at us. The first two hitters in the top of the seventh singled, sharp hits to center field that could have gone for extra bases except for a couple of great throws to the cutoff man. Skip had seen enough. We all had. Skip called time and went to the mound.

"Art, I'm bringing Jorge in," he said.

"Okay, Skip," Art responded, looking crushed. "Sorry I couldn't close it out for us."

"You did great. We'll win this one." Skip said as Art headed to the dugout. When Jorge trotted in from the bullpen, Skip handed him the ball and said, "First and second, no one out. Go get 'em!"

Jorge was throwing big-time heat. He struck out the first two batters he faced. Then he got wild--maybe he was trying to be a little too perfect. He ending up hitting the next batter, who we all thought was leaning a little too close to the plate. That loaded the bases. Then he walked the next guy on five pitches, which scored a run. Now the score was 8–6, still bases loaded, and two out. Nothing like a two-out rally to get a team fired up.

Skip looked over at me and I said to myself, do what got us here. Don't change now!

Finally, he went out to talk to Jorge, and the rest of the infield joined him. "How do you feel?" he asked.

"Great," Jorge replied. "Sorry 'bout those last two guys."

Then Skip took the unusual step of waving me in from the outfield. "Dave," Skip asked, studying me, "how's your arm?"

"Fine."

"Want in?"

I shrugged my shoulders. I meant what I said before the game—I wanted the other guys to get their chance, too. And I wanted it for Jorge. He was a good guy and he deserved that feeling of being on top of the world.

"Your call" Skip said.

"Okay," he said, thinking it over, glancing at Jorge. I guess some managerial sixth sense told him Jorge still had something left in the tank.

"Jorge, go get 'em!" he said. He gave me a knowing glance, as if to say, be ready to pitch.

From that point on, Jorge did not disappoint anyone, especially himself. Strike one… strike two…ball one, wasting a pitch low and outside to see if the hitter would reach for it, which he didn't…and then strike three! Inning over. Way to go, Jorge! He was mobbed in the dugout, and the fans gave him a standing ovation.

Then, Skip told me to go warm up a little more. "You're pitching the eighth and ninth. Time to take it home, Dave!"

When I ran down to the bull pen, along the right field line the fans went wild, screaming, "Dave, Dave, Dave!"

I told Rocky, our catcher to go to my curveball in the top of the eighth, and to the fastball in the ninth. Rocky was big, tough, hustling Italian from northern New Jersey who was in his second year with the team and was very popular with the fans. "It's your time," he said, slapping me on the shoulder. "Close it out and take us home!"

"You got it, Rock."

My curveball was un-hittable—two strikeouts on six straight curveballs, then a weak comebacker to the mound, which I grabbed, took a couple of steps toward first, and threw underhand to our first baseman to get the third out.

With the score 8–6 in the bottom of the eighth, we scored another run. Skip hit a towering opposite-field home run over the left-field wall—impressively, his thirty-ninth for the season. It was the top of the ninth and we were three outs away from locking up a tie for first place. We were winning 9–6.

Before I went to the mound, I walked toward Skip.

"Before bedlam breaks out," I told him, "I want to tell you something—this one's for you, Skip, the best manager any player ever had."

He thanked me with a pat on the back, then went back to first base. Now it was just Rocky and me. I stared down at home and locked into my zone—and visualized the strings! I remembered everything Eddie Lopat taught me. Three heaters in the low nineties, one out! Three more heaters in the mid nineties, two out! Three heaters maybe even in the low hundreds, three out!

I dropped to my knees, put my hands over my head, and cried. I had struck out all six batters I faced. We did it. We won, and tied for first place. We were headed to a one-game playoff for the PONY League championship! I kissed the ground and thanked God.

Before I knew what was happening, I was covered with players. Skip, Stoney, and Rocky leaned over me to act as a shield against the chaos.

The fans were totally out of control. It took us ten full minutes to make it to the clubhouse—with a police escort! The fans were still screaming, "Yankees! Yankees! Yankees!" and wouldn't calm down until we came back out to take a bow.

When we did, Mayor Martinson already had a microphone set up at home plate. "Ssshhh…everybody…quiet! Let's take a moment to thank our wonderful Olean Yankees for bringing the championship game home!" he announced. The crowd erupted again. "We have waited a long time for this moment. You're the greatest fans anyone could ask for—and we have the greatest team!" The roar was deafening and seemed to go on forever.

When everyone settled down, the mayor went on. "The one-game playoff for the PONY League championship will take place here on Labor Day, Monday, September fourth. Pre-game ceremonies begin at one o'clock, game time is two. Now, please, everybody, drive home safely."

Back in the clubhouse, things were just as crazy. Everyone was hugging congratulating each other. It was a magical moment in time. Skip was jubilant and he hugged me so hard it hurt.

In the midst of it, we could barely hear the ringing of a telephone. Skip ran to it then called, "Dave, someone wants to talk to you. Take it in my office."

I went in to pick up the phone. "Hello?"

"Dave, congratulations. Great job!" the voice on the other end said. I could barely hear him over the clubhouse noise. I couldn't tell who was speaking.

"We're very proud of you and the team," the voice added.

"Thank you. Who is this?"

"Howie McPherson."

I could hardly believe it. Howie McPherson, the owner of the New York Yankees, was calling me!

"Sorry, sir," I stammered. "I didn't recognize your voice. Thank you, thank you. The whole team did it, though, not just me."

"Good luck Monday. Go get 'em!"

"Thanks again, Mr. McPherson."

"Bye, Dave. See you soon. See you very soon."

"Bye," I said. As I hung up the phone, his final words echoed in my ears. See me very soon? That was a strange thing to say, considering I'd never met the man. Maybe he was coming to the championship game?

CHAPTER 4

The Dirt On Dave Roth

"Welcome back." Fletch was reclining in his leather chair with his feet on his desk. Mac was on the edge of his chair, and Casey kept nervously swishing the scotch around in his glass.

"I take it you've got some news for me." Fletch said.

"Sure do, boss," Casey said.

Fletch asked, "Good or bad?"

Mac and Casey exchanged a look. Fletch grinned, enjoying their uneasiness.

"If it's good, you may have earned a cigar," Fletch said. "If it's bad, then one of you guys better pour me a double, on the double."

Casey cleared his throat and said, "Well, sir…" He gave a tentative glance at Mac, hoping for moral support. "We think it's good, really good."

Casey's words were failing him. He felt a little woozy from the scotch, and Fletch's sarcasm was undermining his thoughts.

Mac saw it and took the ball that Casey was dropping.

"Look, Fletch. Tonight the Olean Yankees won and tied for first place. First time Olean's been headed to a championship play-off since 1923. And you know who we can thank for it? Our boy Dave Roth."

Fletch crossed his arms. "Oh yeah?" he asked, sounding doubtful.

"Yep. The kid threw a curveball that was out of this world. Strikeout after strikeout. I hear the fans never sat down while he was pitching the eighth and ninth—they were going wild."

"Excited fans don't count for much," Fletch said. "That's the Minors. This is THE SHOW!"

Mac shook his head and said, "He struck out five out of six to wrap up the win, and a chance to play for the championship. This kid's a comer. You should hear the way his manager talks about him. Like he's the second coming of Babe Ruth."

Fletch raised his eyebrows and said, "You spoke to his manager?"

"Of course I did!" Casey replied angrily. "You said we oughta do our homework, so when I got word that Olean won, I put a call in to Wally Lance, their manager. He said Dave's the reason for their success this season. Said the kid's got an incredible gift...and he's humble about it, too."

Casey, having recovered his voice, and his thoughts, added, "And his merits are pretty damn meritable!"

"I talked to Dave, too," Mac continued. "A real nice kid. You could tell he never thought he would be talking to the owner of the New York Yankees."

"Careful, Mac," Fletch said, with a sarcastic grin. "Wouldn't want your buttons to pop off your vest."

"The point is that the kid's a shoe-in for the big leagues. Everything he touches turns to gold. Pitching, batting—he can do no wrong." Mac cleared his throat. "That's why he's exactly the player we need to start against the Red Sox. Dave Roth is the best candidate we've got."

"And what else did you find out about him?" Fletch asked.

"Sorry?" Mac responded.

"I told you I wanted the dirt on Dave Roth."

"Oh...right. The dirt on Dave Roth."

Mac looked helplessly at Casey and said, "We've been so focused on Dave's performance on the field, I didn't do any further research".

"He's a good kid," Casey said. "A nice Jewish kid from the South Bronx. Parents still married. Good student at Morris High School. Something about a little gang activity a couple of years ago, but nothing that should cause us any trouble."

"Gang activity?" Mac asked, surprised.

"Sure. But it's the South Bronx. It ain't Scarsdale. Everyone there is part of some kind of gang or social club."

Casey held his breath. In actuality, he hadn't dug too deeply into

Roth's past because he thought Fletch's request was ridiculous. The kid is a damn good ballplayer. What else mattered?

"Well," Fletch said slowly, "it looks like for once, you guys didn't let me down."

Mac slapped his knee in agreement.

"Then it's decided! Olean has their championship game against Jamestown on Monday where I plan on making an appearance myself. I'll tell him after the game," Mac said.

Casey stood up.

"I'd like to go, too, if you don't mind. My coaches can take over for one game," he said.

"Sure, Casey. We'll make a day of it." He turned to Fletch. "Are you up for a road trip?"

"Wish I could. But I've got family plans on Monday, Labor Day."

Fletch shook hands with Casey, then with Mac.

"You won't regret this, Fletch," Mac said, vigorously pumping Fletch's hand. "You've made the right decision. Dave Roth is going to get his shot at greatness. And the Yankees are going to get a new star."

"Let's hope so, Mac," Fletch said. "Let's hope so."

Fletch watched Casey and Mac close the door behind them and hurry down the stairs. He watched them cross past the bleachers and walk down toward the diamond. They got smaller and smaller until they became specks, finally disappearing into the night.

When he was sure he couldn't see them anymore, he swung his feet off the desk, picked up his phone, and dialed a number from memory.

"Romanelli? Get in my office asap. I've got a job for you."

Vince Romanelli was the kind of guy who could make himself disappear. Whether it was a crowded room or a deserted street at midnight, he could vanish effortlessly into his surroundings. He was short with greasy black hair and a bad complexion. There was nothing striking about him. He was a master of the art of being nowhere and everywhere at the same time. What's more, no one could ever pick him out in a police lineup. It was a skill that came in handy with the many varied jobs Vince picked up.

Vince arrived at Fletch's office at the top of Yankee Stadium within the hour, he didn't have to knock. The GM was waiting for him.

"Door's open," he called out. "Come in."

Vince pushed the door open and stepped inside.

"Good to see you, Fletch," he said, his voice low and musical. "It's been a long time."

"Been quite a while. Have a seat, my friend," Fletch added.

Romanelli closed the door behind him and moved silently to a chair. He walked so lightly on his feet that he left no indentations on the plush carpeting. He literally left no trace.

"So, Fletch," he began. "What can I do for you?"

"I need your help with something."

"What's the job? I have stopped taking certain assignments."

"Business wasn't good?" Fletch asked.

"Far from it. Business was too good." Vince said.

"I see." Fletch made an admiring glance at his friend. "You really do have a gift."

"So I've been told." Vince added.

Romanelli took in his surroundings, noting the level of scotch in Fletch's glass and the soft ticking of the grandfather clock in the corner. His skills of observation were unusually keen. Give him thirty seconds in any room and he could sketch it from memory with barely a flaw.

Fletch leaned back in his chair, well aware that Romanelli was memorizing every intricate detail of his office.

"Don't worry. The project I have in mind won't get you into any trouble, legal or otherwise." Fletch said.

"I'm listening." Vince answered.

"I need you to do a little PI work."

"Go on," Vince said.

"I need you to run a background check, so to speak. Dig up a little dirt on someone, Fletch said.

"Who's the mark?"

"His name is Dave Roth." Fletch responded.

"I see." Vince answered.

"Cigar?" Fletch said, opening an expensive box of Cubans.

"No, thanks. I don't smoke on the job."

It was true. Vince never drank or smoke—he felt it impaired his ability to be completely present and alert.

"Is it about your wife?" Romanelli asked.

Fletch chuckled.

"Far from it. There's a better chance of me hitting a home run than the old bag running around on me."

"So this is work related. A manager? A player?" Vince asked.

"A prospective player, yes."

"Got it. So you want the dirt on a player?"

"Yes, that's right," Fletch answered.

Fletch opened a drawer in his desk and pulled out a plain white folder.

"Here's the basics—name, age, and address. He was in a gang in the South Bronx."

"Any idea which one? There's a bunch. I came out of one, myself," Vince responded.

Fletch shrugged. "You're asking me? That's your job to find out."

"Done." Vince reacted.

Vince slipped the folder into his leather jacket, which seemed to swallow it, as he got up.

"I have what I need." Vince said.

"Excellent. How much time, do you think?" Fletch asked.

"A few days. You'll have your dirt by next week." Vince answered.

"Perfect. Do a good job and you'll make your best tip ever." Fletch said.

"You've never let me down so far, boss." Vince said.

"That's because you've never let *me* down, old friend. Nothing personal, but you take off first. I don't want us to be seen together."

Romanelli's eyes lingered on Fletch's face. There was a patchwork of lines and creases that made Fletch look much older than he was. The years have not been kind to him, Vince concluded. The Yankee GM looked more and more like an old man every day.

CHAPTER 5

The Night Before

The Jamestown Tigers had their ace pitcher, John Hare going for them. Hare was a six-foot-two, hard-throwing, right-handed sidearmer who had a reputation for intentionally throwing at key players' heads.

Knocking someone down is part of the game, but trying to hit a batter in the head—and possibly causing permanent damage or even killing him—is just wrong, rotten, and stupid. Hare was known as a madman, for good reason—his antics on the mound were crazy. Once, he'd actually thrown a baseball into the announcer's booth and screamed at Harry Bolton, the Jamestown announcer, "Get in the game, you idiot!" Hare was enraged because Bolton had made a mistake when announcing his stats.

He was downright mean and more than a little dangerous, and that's what worried me. I saw that sort of uncontrolled rage before—I also saw what it could do. Every time I looked at John Hare, I saw a flash of Big Joe O'Neill the night of the rumble. It made my skin crawl.

The night before our championship game against the Tigers, we went to the Tavern for a few beers. Some of the Jamestown players were there. They were good enough guys, friendly and approachable.

It became obvious that most of the Jamestown players weren't so crazy about John Hare, either, they told us he was a bigot. Word on the street was that Hare had some questionable ties with the white supremacist movement back in his Mississippi hometown.

I exchanged glances with C. As the only black guy on our team, C had taken a lot of teasing that summer, some of it friendly and some of it not so friendly. He is a quiet guy from a tough background. He was born Cecil Charles Flood in a tough neighborhood in Oakland, California, one of twelve brothers and sisters. His parents couldn't afford them. The had to give him up to a foster home at the age of nine.

C was put in the care of a childless white couple, Wilma and Joseph Fredrickson, whom he loved as his real parents. They owned a small printing company and raised him well. C excelled in high school, both academically and in sports.

The Yankees had scouted C through high school. They signed him immediately after graduation, in early June. His gift on the field was undeniable. Skip told me this story about him early on, and I thought of it from time to time—especially at moments like this, when circumstances brought unwanted attention to race and religion.

Suddenly, Stoney tapped C and me on the shoulder. "Look who just walked in."

Hare and Miller, Jamestown's catcher, walked directly over to the bar, right near us, and ordered two beers. Then Hare turned and looked right at me.

"Hey, Jew boy, I hear you called me a 'dumb rabbit.'"

I shook my head calmly. "No, I didn't."

"You calling Miller here a liar?"

"If he told you that, then yes, I am." I put myself into a position to handle anything Hare wanted to try, stepping out in front of C.

"Hear that, Miller?" Hare asked his friend.

"Sure did, roomie," Miller replied. "Doesn't surprise me, though. Jews are known to be yellow liars!"

I wanted to clock the both of them, I held my temper back. "Would you like to know what I really said?" I angrily asked him.

"Yeah," Hare barked.

"I didn't say you were a 'dumb rabbit,' I told him, you're a 'dumb idiot, low-life rotten rabbit.' And that's even worse than being a gutless moron like Miller."

I could see Hare beginning to fume. His face was turning red as he stared daggers at me. "You kikes and niggers don't belong in a white man's game!" he said, practically foaming at the mouth.

I stepped closer to him. "What did you just say?" I asked.

"You heard me. You think I'm a dumb low-life bunny? Well you're a dumb bagel-doggin' kike," Hare said.

Just then, Skip stepped in. The crowd grabbed Hare and Miller, ushering them outside before things got out of hand. I followed behind.

"Don't come back," Skip told the two of them. "If you do, we'll let Dave loose on you!"

Skip didn't know much about my gang history, but he must have sensed I could be very physical and take care of myself.

Man, did I want a piece of them! If they so much as set foot in here again, I decided to knock 'em both on their butts.

The air was tense, but the whole place seemed to loosen up when Rocky, in an innocent tone, said, "He really is a dumb idiot bunny!" With that, we all ordered another round.

We ate light that night, just burgers and fries instead of the usual steaks. When Skip left, the six of us decided to go for a ride in Stoney's car. It was sad because we knew it was probably the last time all of us would be together after tomorrow's game.

After driving around a bit, we dropped Bobby, Dean, and Candle off at home. Then Stoney took C home, and I went for the ride. C was even angrier than I was about Hare and Miller's bigot remarks, and I was concerned he would go to the Olean Hotel to look for them once we dropped him off. On the way to his place, I tried to calm him down.

"Please, C," I said, "stay home tonight and get some rest—then get four hits for us tomorrow. That's the best way to deal with those bigots."

He thought for a second then said, "Okay, Dave," sounding less upset. "As long as you're all right."

"I am," I assured him.

I smiled as C got out of the car and headed upstairs to his room. But as I watched him go, I realized Hare had managed to tap into a deep rage bubbling inside me, something I thought I had managed to bury.

THE NIGHT BEFORE

❖ ❖ ❖

That night I couldn't sleep.

"Candle, you awake?" I asked.

"Si," came his reply.

When Candle had first arrived from Venezuela in June, he'd hardly spoken any English. Now, over two months later, his English was practically better than mine. My Spanish wasn't too shabby, either. Somehow, learning Spanish made me feel closer to Irena. Of course deep down I knew nothing I did would ever bring her back.

I looked at my alarm clock. It was two in the morning.

"I'm going to take a walk," I said to Candle as I put on my sneakers.

"Donde?" Candle asked.

"To the ballpark," I said, the idea just coming to me. "Wanna come?"

He threw back his bedcovers. "Si, mi amigo. No puedo dormir." "I can't sleep either."

It was a beautiful night outside. The forecast for Labor Day called for very hot, Indian summer weather.

What a showcase it'll be, the ballpark will be packed. A special section was built to accommodate scouts and special guests—practically every Major League team would be represented. Wow, it's going to be exciting!

I thought about my future. After the game, I would be heading back to the Bronx. It would be good to see my buddies again and to spend time with Mom and Dad, who were excited about having their son back for a while. But I worried about the lingering murder charges and having to face the music in court. And there was another worry, too, one that the confrontation with Hare had brought to the surface. I couldn't help but wonder if being back in my old hood would stir up old trouble. Word had it that Alejandro was out of jail and thirsty for vengeance. And if I ever saw Big Joe O'Neill's face, I had no way of predicting just what I would do.

Candle and I walked in silence. We became close that summer, roommates and blood brothers. He was the only one of my teammates who I told about my past. I trusted him with my life.

After we walked without saying anything for a long while, I said, "Candle, you're like a brother to me. I'm going to miss you."

"I'm going to miss you too, my friend."

"How are you getting home?" I asked.

"First, a bus to Binghamton. Then a plane to Nueva York and another plane to Miami. A short time there then TWA takes me to Caracas. My family will meet me at the aeropuerto."

"Long trip," I said.

Candle nodded. "What about your plans? How will you get home?"

"I bus it to Buffalo at nueve, then a train to Nueva York's Penn Station, where Dad'll meet me. And then the Lexington Avenue subway to the South Bronx."

I paused. "I'm scared about going back," I admitted in a quiet voice.

Candle placed a hand on my shoulder. "I understand, Dave. You have a lot of darkness waiting because of your old life. I've seen you grow strong and confident this summer, and gang life had nothing to do with it. Tonight you showed great self-restraint. You are a good and honest man, and no matter what lies ahead, you'll be able to handle it."

I smiled gratefully at my friend. "I think my English is getting better just listening to you. Gracias." I told him.

Looking around at the ballpark, I said, "Only sixty feet, six inches from the pitcher's mound...to home plate...to history!" I thought again about Candle's kind words. "I know I can do this. I feel totally focused on the game."

Then, an idea hit me. I reached into my pocket, pulled something out and showed it to Candle. "Here—this is my lucky penny. I would like you to have it."

Candle took the penny and examined it, turning it over in his hand a few times. "Thank you," he said. "I've never seen a silver penny. Is it real?"

"It's not silver, it's zinc-coated steel. In 1943, our government needed copper for the war effort. So, that year only, pennies were made of steel. It happened once in a lifetime, just like this season."

The Night Before

Candle tossed the coin into the air and caught it again, gripping it in his fist. "I have an idea," he said. "Let's hop the fence and bury it in the pitcher's mound. It will be our bond and always remind us of this special year."

I grinned. I loved the idea! "Man, let's do that!" I said. We helped each other hop over the outfield fence and made our way to the pitcher's mound. It was creepy, being on the field in the middle of the night.

"Let's dig a hole right here with our fingers," Candle said. Just as I bent down, he added, "Dave, use your left hand."

"Yes, Mom," I joked.

We began to dig under the rubber strip on the mound. When we had a small but deep hole, we put the penny in and covered it up again with dirt.

"There," I said. "Done. No one will ever know about it but us."

As we stood there in silence, I surveyed the field again. "None of this feels real. Candle, do you think maybe it was all a dream?"

He laughed a little but didn't answer, even though I didn't expect him to.

We were at peace with ourselves, our friendship was stronger than ever, and the future—at least the part of it I could see—seemed bright. "We should probably go back and get some sleep, amigo," I said. "Tomorrow, we go to battle."

CHAPTER 6

The Championship Game

"Ladies and gentlemen, this is Jeff Walters, your Olean Yankees radio announcer for WOLA, 600 on your AM dial. It's a big day here in Olean!"

"We have Dave Roth with us for a few minutes before he warms up," Jeff continued. "He's the starting pitcher today."

"How do you feel?" Jeff asked.

"Great." I answered.

"Are you nervous?"

"About what?" I said.

"John Hare. He's got a reputation for being a loose cannon."

"Nothing to be nervous about," I said nonchalantly.

Jeff said. "Ladies and gentlemen, we are talking to Dave Roth, who is all business. Tell me, Dave, why are you wearing a blue bandana under your cap?"

"In the South Bronx," I replied, "we wear these for rumbles or stickball games."

"Well, this is certainly going to be a rumble today!" Jeff agreed.

"It's just a game," I said, grinning. "But it's a game we really want to win!"

Jeff grinned back. "That's the spirit! Thanks and good luck."

With that, I stood up and headed to take some BP.

Candle was right, I thought to myself as I jogged to the bull pen to warm up. I have come a long way.

"Dave!"

I looked up to see Skip calling me. I ran over to him.

"I'm going to give you some serious advice," he said. "Don't ruin a

The Championship Game

great season or even a career because of two idiots." He looked toward Hare and Miller. "Stoney told me what you told C last night. Take your own advice, Dave. Four for four from C and a complete game shutout from you would be the best way to shut them up!"

I smiled. "You got it, Skip!"

Skip couldn't help smiling, too, although he was serious. "Dave, you're one of the best all-around athletes I've ever seen or had the pleasure of playing with. You're a genuine team player—and that's even more rare. I don't know much about your past, but I know you've got a great future in this game. So don't ruin it now."

The smile went away as he continued. "Hare and Miller will do and say everything they can to rattle you, especially when you're at bat. No matter what happens, be selfish today. The win is for the team, but pitch this one for Dave!"

"Yes, sir," I replied.

"One more thing besides that, soldier," Skip said. He leaned in closer to me, a very stern look on his face. "You're a Jew bum and I wish someone would cut your tail and horns off. You're also a nigger lover and a jerk!" He stared me in the eye, and I glared right back. I was shocked he would say that to me. That wasn't the Skip I knew. He would never—

Then it hit me. He wasn't insulting me. He was preparing me.

"Sir," I said loudly, as if I really were a soldier responding to my drill sergeant. "Thank you for my basic training, sir!"

Skip smiled. "Now go get 'em, soldier."

All the players and coaches from both teams were introduced. The national anthem was played and them we heard those familiar words from the home plate umpire, "Play ball!"

As we came to bat in the bottom half of the first inning, there was no score. I struck out all three batters in the top of the first. The Tigers took the field, their confidence shaken up a little bit by my pitching, as Hare took his final warm-up pitches.

Leading off for Olean was our outstanding second baseman, Bobby Richardson, who was very popular—that was evident from the roar of the fans. He was also a great guy and a spiritual person who exuded a calming influence in the clubhouse and a great roommate.

Bobby dug in, a fastball right down the middle. Bobby jumped on it—a line drive right at Jeffries, the third baseman. That was one out.

Candle was up next, hitting from the left side. He was a hitting machine! Candle swung at the first pitch—a high, high fly ball to Overton, the center fielder, for the second out.

Hitting third, from the left side, was the ever-popular Stoney Smith. Hare, a right-handed pitcher, delivered a big side-arm curveball for strike one. Next pitch, ball one. The fans were all over Hare—this guy was nobody's favorite—but he seemed to be handling their razzing pretty well.

Stoney swung at the next pitch—strike two. Then a fastball, low, on the outside corner, for strike three and the third out. Hare had set us down in one-two-three fashion, paying us back for the one-two-three inning in the top of the first.

"Hey, this is gonna be a pitcher's duel for the ages!" Jeff announced to the radio listeners. I had a feeling he'd be right.

At the top of the second, I noticed that the scouts were looking at each other in amazement—and at the radar guns, these huge contraptions the size of movie cameras used to record the speed of each pitch. Even Mac and Casey were looking at each other with big smiles on their faces. As I later found out, they were consistently clocking me at ninety-eight to a hundred and two miles per hour.

In the announcer's booth, Jeff said, "Harry, I've never seen fastballs like this!"

"Neither have I!" said Harry. "I just wish it wasn't against my team."

The Championship Game

"Unbelievable!" Jeff yelled into his microphone. "Eighteen pitches, six strikeouts! Does he have good stuff or what? I mean, folks, he's got stuff like I've never seen!"

The Tigers took the field again. I went to my corner of the dugout and stared at Hare. I hoped he knew that I meant business, because I did. I was done playing around with him!

With one out in the bottom of the second, hitting fifth, C stepped in and took ball one, which was high and very tight. It pushed him back pretty good.

Ball two, also high and tight, just about knocked C down. He had a very determined look on his face as he was staring at Hare. It was obvious there was no love lost between these guys.

Next came a fastball, and C slammed it right through Hare's legs for the first hit of the game. It was clear he was hitting through the middle, and Hare was his target. C was on first with one out.

Rocky was next, he stepped up to the plate, the fans were chanting, "Rocky! Rocky! Rocky!" He took strike one, then swung and missed the next pitch. The bat flew out of his hand and toward the mound. It didn't hit anyone, but you could cut the tension with a knife.

All of us in the dugout were on our feet, ready to jump in, but I looked at each of the guys as if to say, "Stay loose—remember your promise. Remember the promise you made to me before the game." They all looked back at me, and at each other, then sank onto the bench.

Jerry retrieved Rocky's bat. He took the next pitch for strike three, and two out.

In the seven hole was Dean, he stepped in on the right side and Hare delivered his first pitch. Dean dragged a bunt down the third-base line, and it looked great! Jefferies bare-handed the ball and threw to first, but not in time. Dean had beaten it out for a hit.

We had two outs, C on second and Dean on first.

"Olean is threatening," Jeff noted, "with Eddie Rippili coming up."

Eddie stepped in, hitting from the right side, he was a terrific, versatile fielding talent, but not the greatest hitter, however, he had mastered the art of the push-bunt, which was when the batter bunted and tried to make the second baseman field it. If he could get the ball past the pitcher, it was almost a guaranteed hit, and this was the perfect time to do it. If Eddie can get on, I'm on deck, I thought.

Eddie took ball one, then ball two. Hare had thrown a lot of pitches that inning. The next pitch, Eddie pushed a bunt to second base. It was perfect—Brandson had no chance. Dean was running the moment the ball was bunted.

"Well, Harry," Jeff said, sitting back in his chair in the announcer's booth. "We've got two outs, bases loaded, in the bottom of the second. Dave's up next, hitting from the right side, he's one of the main reasons why Olean is in this championship play-off game. He's had a dream season so far, but it won't be complete without a win today."

I stepped in. Miller, the catcher, was mouthing off as usual, but I aimed all my attention at Hare. He was my focus, and he stared back just as intently.

"Hey, Jew boy," Miller yelled. "You're going down!"

His first pitch knocked me down. The fans were completely silent, but the Olean bench was ready to explode. I got up and brushed myself off. Jamestown's manager was yelling, "Hare, you better not walk him!" He sounded furious.

The next pitch missed my head by inches, and I went down again—ball two. Okay, rabbit, I thought. Let's get serious. I decided, then and there, to take one for the team.

Hare threw a side-arm curve and, this time, I didn't go down. I let the pitch hit me in the back. Trying not to show how much pain I felt, I went to first while C scored from third, bringing the score to 1–0.

Back at home plate, Miller and Hare were arguing with the umpire. "He could've gotten out of the way!" Hare shouted.

Miller agreed, "Come on, Blue! He let it hit him!"

The umpire wanted no part of their banter and calmly went about his business, brushing off home plate—with his butt to the pitcher's mound. I guess that showed Hare what the ump thought of his argument.

Seeing I was okay, the fans began to laugh at the scene Hare and Miller were creating. Doc came to first with the old reliable can of spray Freeze-It. I pulled up my shirt and he froze the area where I'd been hit.

Skip came over as well. "You okay?" he asked.

"Yes, sir!"

"Okay, soldier," Skip responded, pleased with my answer. "I think you started something. Go get 'em!"

By the sixth inning, we were up, 6-0. I was pitching a no-hitter. I went out to the mound to a huge roar of approval and gave the fans a wink.

I took my warm-ups then waved Rocky over. "All curveballs this inning."

"Okay, Dave…You the man!"

"Don't get soft on me now, Rock! Let's win this…then I'll give you a big smooch."

"No way, José!"

Miller came up with one out and Hare on deck. Hare was talking to Miller in the on-deck circle. Good luck, guys, I thought. Just try and stop me now.

"Okay, Miller," the umpire yelled, "let's go. Play ball!"

Strike one then strike two.

Hare yelled, "What the hell are you doing?" and I guessed that whatever scheme they'd cooked up, Miller was not sticking to it.

Then Miller tried to bunt with two strikes! He was totally squared around and I delivered a nasty, hard curve. He foul tipped the ball, which was an automatic strike three. The ball ricocheted off the bat and hit him in the jaw. In short, he was out cold.

Doc went to help, but Miller appeared to be okay. I couldn't help but smile when I thought of how tough and cocky Miller had acted the night before standing beside Hare at the Tavern. He didn't look so tough laid out on his back with Doc sticking smelling salts up his nose.

Miller left the game rubbing his jaw, and the umpire announced that Kevin Jones would replace him behind the plate.

Now it was Hare's turn. I threw him nasty curveballs for strikes one and two. The next one was going to have to be something special. Ball one, high and tight, and Hare was on his butt. With ball two, he was down again. He got up glaring at me like he wanted to hit my head with the bat. Then came strike three. How sweet it is! Another inning over.

As we headed to the dugout, the championship in sight, the fans were cheering us on like crazy. But I was staring at Hare, who was still standing there, as if to tell him, "Soon, you'll get what you deserve."

When I got to the dugout, Rocky was already sitting in our usual corner spot.

"Hey, how'd you do that?" he asked. "A strikeout and knockout all in one pitch?"

I smiled. "We're the Team of Destiny, remember? Perhaps a little divine intervention."

"The Team of Destiny," he repeated, softly.

And we really were.

Finally, we reached the top of the ninth, and the score was 7 to 0, Olean. Before the inning started, Mayor Martinson and Chief Whalen walked up to home plate, where a microphone had been set up.

The mayor spoke, smelling the win, "Hello, you wonderful Olean fans! As your mayor, on behalf of Chief Whalen and the Yankees players and management, I'm asking you to please listen carefully. In the event that your Olean Yankees hold the lead—" To this, the crowd responded with an outrageous roar and the mayor had to wait for them to quiet down.

"When they do, we must have calm and order," he went on. "We don't want anyone hurt. Absolutely no one is allowed on the field. If you do come on the field, you will be arrested. After the

The Championship Game

game, the players will be escorted to their respective clubhouses by Chief Whalen's men. They will come back out after a short time to take their bows and receive their awards, presented by league commissioner Randy Briggs. The players will be happy to sign autographs and answer questions at that time—only if we have your cooperation."

A huge wave of applause and agreement filled the ballpark.

The umpire shouted, "Play ball!" and the game resumed once more.

I took my warm-ups and called Rocky out to the mound. "Rock, you caught a great game, plus two home runs," I said. "What a day it's been for all of us. I'll never forget you, my teammate and friend."

"Okay, don't get soft on me now," Rocky replied. "Knock 'em dead this inning—then I'll give you that big smooch I promised ya!"

We both laughed then got down to business. "You call 'em, Rocky. Sit on the fastball. Let's do it!"

"I'm with you!" Rocky said.

Kevin Jones, the Jamestown catcher who had come in for Miller, came to bat with one out. Rumor had it he was a good fastball hitter. I threw a curveball off the table for strike one. I threw another curveball off the table for ball one, then three more for ball two, ball three and strike two. I shook Rocky off and delivered another off-the-table curveball, which he popped up to Richardson. The fans were going wild. We were about to win this thing.

Johnny Templeton, a pinch hitter, and a real speedster came to bat. He was the potential final out. I glared at Rocky's glove then threw a fastball well over 100 on the radar gun for strike one, and another for strike two.

I stepped off the mound and looked into the dugout toward Skip. He saluted me and mouthed the words, "Take it home!"

I threw an Eddie Lopat-style change-up curveball that fell off the table and froze Templeton for strike three, three outs. Game over. We were champions. My God, I felt like I was dreaming.

my first thought was that lucky penny Candle I had buried in the mound had sure done the trick!

The cheering in the stands was thunderous and the fans were jumping up out of their seats. But no one was charging onto the field. They were going wild, but in control.

My God…I just pitched a shutout no-hitter. Wow! I never believed this would or could happen to me or anyone else. I also couldn't believe what the team had done all season. I thanked God for these wonderful teammates of mine, my friends who had helped me make a dream come true. I came a long way from the South Bronx—from my former life. I thought of Irena and how proud she would be of me. And right then, standing on the pitcher's mound surrounded by the team I loved, having just played the game I loved, I had never been so proud of myself.

Out of the corner of my eye, I could see Hare, hands on hips, staring at us from the visitor's dugout. Tough crap, Hare, I thought…We won—You lost!

CHAPTER 7

Playing With The Big Boys

The clubhouse was a madhouse. Everyone was hugging each other, and beer was flowing like a waterfall.

When we all finally calmed down, Skip said, "Listen up, guys. Before we go back out on the field to thank the fans, I want to say a few words. I feel like we came, we saw and we conquered—as a team! This has been a successful season, and you'll all be rewarded greatly for being a part of it. You'll never be forgotten—the record book will always tell the story of the Team of Destiny and what we've accomplished, starting on June 28 and climaxing on September 4, in a little old town in upstate New York called Olean. You'll tell your children and grandchildren all about the summer of 1953. And when you do, always remember there is no 'I' in the word 'team.' It has truly been an honor, gentlemen."

With that, Skip took the time to come over to each of us individually and give us a hug and a firm handshake. We were laughing, crying, and carrying on.

"Hey, Dave, where's that smooch you promised me?" Rocky asked, making everyone laugh, as usual.

"Okay, Rocky, come here," I said, opening my arms to him.

"No way, José!" he said, ducking out of the way.

"Hey, guys!" I said, shouting to make my voice heard above the noise. "I have something I wanna say."

"Go for it, Dave!" someone yelled from the back.

"Thank you," I said "For not letting that bigot Hare ruin our day. I can't tell you how much it means to me to be a part of this team—a team of good guys who know how to stand up for each other like brothers."

I got a little choked up but continued.

"I'm honored to have been the only Jewish ballplayer in this entire league—and I'm especially grateful to all of you for the way I've been accepted and treated. I truly love you guys and thank you a thousand times for allowing me to be part of the team."

I looked around the room and saw nothing but smiles.

"Three cheers for our boy Dave!" Skip yelled, and the room erupted into a hearty round of "hip hip hoorays."

Suddenly, Shultzy charged into the clubhouse.

"Listen up, guys!" he hollered. "This announcement is very important. Everything I'm about to tell you is mandatory."

The team gathered around Shultzy and listened intently.

"First," Shultzy began, glancing at his notes, "no one is going home."

"Second, all new travel arrangements to your destinations will be made for you by the New York Yankees front office."

Wow, I thought, and waited anxiously to hear what was next.

"Third, we will leave the clubhouse on our team bus at 10:00 a.m. on Wednesday for the Bronx. Tuesday, you will all have a day off to recollect your personal items, say your goodbyes, and anything else you've got to do. Sunday, you will be leaving from New York to your destinations."

The Bronx! I couldn't believe it. This news was getting better and better every minute.

"Fourth," Shultzy continued, "we will be staying at the Concourse Plaza in the Bronx, a first-class hotel that's a hop, skip, and a jump from Yankee Stadium. In fact, many of the Yankees live there during the season."

I held my breath, waiting for the rest.

"Fifth, the New York Yankees come home from Cleveland this week. As you all know, they've got a big game against the Boston Red Sox next week. We'll work out with the Yankees on Thursday and Friday…and then, on Saturday, we're going to play them a four-inning exhibition game at noon."

At that point, bedlam broke out. The hootin' and hollerin' got out of control. We were all in a state of delirious happiness. We were going to play the New York Yankees!

"Listen up, that's not all," Shultzy yelled over our celebratory shouting. "When we go to the stadium, jackets and ties are required."

"After the game," Shultzy was saying, "we'll be the guests of Yankee management for a dinner in the main ballroom of the Concourse Plaza, at which time everyone will get a five hundred dollar bonus check as a 'thank you' for setting an example for the entire Minor League system, and for a job well done."

"This is better than my honeymoon!" Rocky yelled. "But please don't tell my wife I said that!" His reply put all of us in a state of hysteria.

"Let's go enjoy our victory, guys," Skip said, corralling the troops. "And let's share it with the best fans in baseball!"

We jogged happily out of the clubhouse to the stadium, where Mayor Martinson gave us a rousing introduction: "Ladies and gentlemen, our Olean Yankees, the PONY League champs!"

The cheering was incredible, even though half the ballpark had emptied out—the Jamestown fans had left.

The Olean High School band was playing "Take Me Out to the Ball Game" as we walked along the box seats signing autographs and went into the stands to shake hands. The fans were so enthusiastic and were trying to get their programs signed by as many players as possible.

"Folks, listen up," Mayor Martinson announced. "I want to thank you for your wonderful cooperation and I'd like to share some great news I just heard. Our Olean Yankees have been invited to play the New York Yankees in an exhibition game at the one and only Yankee Stadium."

The roar was thunderous, so loud that after several minutes, the league commissioner had to quiet everyone so that he could present us with the PONY League championship trophy!

When he did, Skip humbly took the microphone.

"On behalf of the Olean Yankees," he said, "I'd like to give this beautiful trophy to Mayor Martinson, to be placed in City Hall for all time and for all to see, as a thank you to our great Olean fans. It's their trophy!"

The fans went nuts!

More and more news reporters and photographers were showing up every minute it seemed, and flashbulbs were popping all over the place. It was a strange feeling, like being watched by a hundred eyes.

"Dave, Dave," I heard an unfamiliar voice behind me. "I'm Sandy Abrams with the Associated Press," she said.

Sandy wasn't like any reporter I'd ever seen. She was about five-seven, lean, with long, straight blonde hair, piercing blue eyes, and a stunning face. She looked like she could be a movie star.

"Hi, Sandy," I replied, searing for the right words.

"Hiya back," Sandy said. "How does it feel?"

"How does what feel?"

"The game you just pitched…a no-hit shutout and struck out twenty-one batters! Wow!"

"You mean the game we just won? I just happened to be on the mound. Any one of our pitchers would have pitched a winning game."

Sandy nodded at me, scribbled some notes in a pad, and ran off to find another player to interview. I watched her go, trying not to let my eyes linger on her tan and perfectly toned legs.

"Dave!"

Another female voice called out to me. I turned around to see Debbie, our favorite waitress from the Olean Diner. The Diner had become our second home over the course of the season. It was a cool hangout spot, with little five-cent jukeboxes on the walls that had every new song you could think of. I always noticed Debbie standing behind the counter, watching me with a shy smile on her face. She was pretty and I had even nursed a bit of a crush on her all summer, but we never exchanged more words than, "I'll have scrambled eggs and toast, please."

"Hey, Dave," she said. "You were great. Would you sign my program for my little brother? He's a big fan of the Olean Yankees—especially you."

"Sure," I said with a smile, then took her program and began to sign it. "Is he here?"

"Oh, yes."

"Call him over." I said.

"Alexander!" she called, as a ten-year-old boy came running over.

"Pleased to meet you, Mr. Roth," he said, holding out a hand for me to shake.

"Please, call me Dave," I replied, taking his hand. "Do you play baseball?"

"Little League. I wish I could be as good as you, Dave."

"Work hard and you'll be better than me, Alexander. This is for you," I said, holding out the program. "And if you go see that man over there"—I pointed to Shultzy—"he'll give you a PONY League baseball, too, signed by the whole team." I'd arranged to have a few of them on hand as gifts for special fans.

Alexander's eyes lit up. "Thank you!" he said then turned to Debbie. "You're right, sis—he is beautiful."

She blushed, her brother had let the cat out of the bag. I wondered what I would have done with the information her brother spilled if I had known earlier in the summer.

Suddenly I saw Skip waving his arms frantically in the air.

"Dave!" he called. He was standing on the other side of the field with two men in nice black suits. From where I stood, I didn't recognize them. But Skip seemed excited, so I thought I'd better get there fast.

I smiled at Debbie.

"Will I see you at the Tavern later?"

"Sure, Dave," she said softly, "If you'll be there."

"You bet," I said.

When I got to Skip, he was beaming. Now that I had a closer look at the two nicely dressed men, I thought they definitely looked familiar. But where had I seen them? I knew I saw their faces before, but I couldn't remember where...

"Dave," Skip said, breathless. "I would like to introduce you to Howie McPherson, the owner of the New York Yankees, and Casey Stengel, the team's manager. I couldn't believe Mr. McPherson and Mr. Stengel came to see our game. Wow!

Suddenly it all clicked. I was standing in front of two legends! I knew both of their faces from the newsreels. It was unbelievable to meet them in person.

"Pleased to meet you both," I stammered, suddenly feeling very underdressed in my sweaty uniform.

"The pleasure is ours, Dave," Mac said. "We spoke on the phone a few days ago, but it's nice to meet you in person."

"Mr. McPherson and Mr. Stengel, they made the trip from New York to see you play." Skip said.

"Wow," I said, truly honored. "I don't know what to say."

"You've had a storybook season, Dave," Casey said. "And today's game was the icing on the cake. You pitched a historic game."

"You've got exactly the kind of stuff we are looking for," Mac said.

I looked from Mr. Stengel to Mr. McPherson, than back to Skip. I wasn't sure I understood what was going on.

"How would you feel about pitching in Yankee Stadium?" Mac asked.

"I feel great about it, sir," I said. "We're all excited about going to New York. And I couldn't be more excited about the exhibition game. Playing against the New York Yankees is a dream come true."

Mac and Casey exchanged a glance.

"How about playing with the Yankees...and pitching against the Red Sox instead?" Casey asked.

"I'm sorry," I said, shaking my head. "I'm not sure I understand what you mean."

"You've been called up, Dave," Skip said, unable to contain his excitement any longer. "You're on the roster for the Red Sox-Yankee game next week! You're getting the start!"

"I'm on the roster…" All I could do was repeat what they said.

"You're pitching for the New York Yankees. You just made baseball history," Mac said.

I heard the words come out of his mouth with my own ears, but I still couldn't believe it.

"I'm pitching…for the New York Yankees? Straight out of Class 'D'?" I gulped.

"That's right, Dave," Mac said, patting me on the back. "You're going to THE SHOW!"

CHAPTER 8
Victory Night

I'm still numb from the game and the good news I got from Mr. McPherson and Mr. Stengel. I headed to the Tavern to meet up with the rest of the team.

Mr. Stengel was right—I'd had a storybook season. But that was with Olean, a Minor League team. Pitching for the New York Yankees was a whole other ball game.

I can't wait to share the good news with Mom and Dad. They'll be thrilled. I'm sure they'll call in the morning.

Tonight is for celebration.

I pushed through the swinging doors of the Tavern and was not surprised to see the place packed. Fortunately, there was a roped-off area for the team and press. I found Candle and we ordered a couple of beers. I didn't tell him or anyone else about being called up to the "The Show" —it wasn't the right time. I didn't want it to be about me, this season was an incredible team effort.

Then I saw Debbie, lovely as ever, drinking a soda pop alone.

"I'm going to walk around and say hello to some of our friends," I told Candle.

"Me, too," Candle said. We agreed to meet up again later for another beer. Then I pushed through a wall of people to get to the one person I really wanted to say hello to.

Debbie's eyes lit up when she saw me.

"Thanks for being so kind to my little brother today, Dave," she said. "That autographed ball meant the world to him. He really likes you."

"You're welcome," I told her. "And how about you?"

She looked puzzled. "Me? I don't understand."

"Do you like me?"

She smiled. "Yes, very much. Would you like to dance?" She asked.

"Sure, I'd love to dance. In New York City, I used to go to the Y dances on Sunday afternoons—first a basketball game, then a dance."

I took her hand and led her over to the area where everyone was dancing. Then I heard what was playing: "Earth Angel."

"Is this okay?" I asked.

She shrugged her shoulders. "Why are you asking?"

"Well…we'll get pretty close if we slow dance."

She smiled again. "That's good."

I took her in my arms as we began to sway back and forth, hedged in tightly by all the people around us. We were very close as she pressed her cheek to mine. I could feel her warm breath on my neck.

"You know, Dave," she said, whispering into my ear, "What my brother said is true. I really think you're beautiful."

"Hardly," I said, my mouth almost touching her ear. "I'm just a lucky guy dancing with a beautiful girl." I could feel Debbie's breasts pressed up against my chest. They were very full and firm. It's been a long, long time since I felt a woman that close to me.

"I wish we'd gotten a chance to know each other better this summer," she said. "And now you're leaving."

"I know," I said. "I've been admiring you from a distance since I got here in June. Every time we would go to the diner, I secretly hoped you would be our waitress. For some reason, I never got up the nerve to ask you out."

Debbie blushed.

"I wish you would have, Dave."

"If I'd known you were interested, I would have…"

"Do you want to go for a ride later?" she murmured.

"Sure." I said.

"How about seven?" she asked. "I'll go home and get my car, and pick you up out front. It'll be nice to get away from the crowd for a little while."

The song was coming to an end. Lucky thing, too, because everything was getting little too hot!

VICTORY NIGHT

"See you at seven. And save me a dance for later," she whispered, as she moved away from me and back into the crowd.

I needed a cold beer to cool me down. I went to find Candle and we had another one together.

"Good night for you, Dave?" Candle asked.

I grinned and said, "Yes, so far."

"Dave? Dave?"

As if on cue, the attractive reporter from the Associated Press came toward me from the crowd. Candle saw someone he knew on the other side of the room and excused himself.

"Sandy Abrams," she said as she approached me, and continued. "Don't worry, I don't want an interview."

"Isn't that what you reporters do?" I teased.

"Most of the time," she said. "But I'm not like any reporter you'll ever meet." She gave me an inviting look. "I want a whole lot more from you than an interview."

I was taken back by how aggressive she was. It was almost a little scary...but very sexy.

"Then what do you want?" I asked.

"I'm only interning with the AP for the summer. I happened to have been in the area, visiting friends for the weekend, when my boss sent me a message to get here immediately—that baseball history was being made."

"Okay," I said, wondering where this was going.

"I'm starting my senior year at Columbia. My dream is to be a sports reporter or broadcaster."

"That's great, Sandy," I said. "Good female sports reporters are rare."

"Thanks," she said. "But I need your help."

I paused, looking at her. "Me? Why?"

"Yes, you. I know you're going back to New York. Let's meet up there. I want to do a feature cover story about you for *Look* magazine."

"Wow," I said, not knowing quite what to say. "I'm flattered. But... I'm not sure I could handle that kind of attention."

"I understand," she said. But Sandy didn't seem like the type of girl to take no for an answer. "Well, how about just spending the day talking to me? Or we can talk over dinner, then if you say 'no', it's fine. Dinner's still on me."

I thought about it for a moment then nodded. "That sounds okay." I thought for another moment. "Do you really think you can get me on the cover of *Look*?"

Sandy laughed. "My dad's the President and Publisher! That's not a guarantee, but you'll surely get a fair shot—maybe a little more than fair."

I laughed, too, not having expected an answer like that at all. "Abrams, huh? Are you Jewish?"

"Yes, we're Reformed Jews. Why?"

"Me too. I was Orthodox and kosher until I came to Olean."

"Please, Dave?" she asked. "It would help me out a lot, and I'd be very grateful to you."

Man, I thought, she's sharp and attractive. This could be fun. I said, "It would be my pleasure to help a young, aspiring Jewish sports journalist. How does that sound?"

"Sounds great," she said. "I'll be covering your workouts and the game against the Yankees, so I'll catch up with you then and we can make plans to meet, okay?"

"Okay," I replied.

"Thanks, Dave. You're a good guy. I look forward to getting to know you better." She looked like she was going to hug me, but then stuck out her hand for me to shake—a real professional.

"Thanks, Sandy," I said. "Me, too."

When seven o'clock rolled around, I excused myself from my teammates and stepped outside the Tavern. Debbie was waiting in her car.

"Hi, Debbie," I said, jumping into the passenger's seat.

"Hi, Dave." She had changed into a pale green dress that was very low-cut. I tried not to stare to much.

"Where would you like to go?" I asked.

"How about my house?" she offered. "My parents went to Batavia to have dinner with my aunt and uncle. They won't be back until after ten. Alexander is sleeping over at a friend's house. What do you think?"

"Sounds great. I do have to be back at the Tavern at some point so I can spend time with the rest of the guys, but I still would like to have that dance."

"Of course," she said. Her house was only a few blocks down the street.

Debbie's house was nice, but I didn't have much time to look around. As soon as we got in the door, she grabbed me and said, "Kiss me."

Our lips touched and I melted. I hadn't kissed a girl in ages, not since Irena the day she...I tried not to think about it. I pushed it to the back of my mind so that I could enjoy the moment. And enjoy it I did. Debbie's lips were so full and soft. Man, was she hot—and a good kisser!

"Dave," she said after a moment or two. "Let's go upstairs and... dance."

She took me by the hand and led me up to her bedroom, where "Earth Angel" was already on the record player. She obviously had all this planned.

"I guess you want to dance to a slow song?" I asked.

"Yes," she replied, moving close. "I want to be near you."

"Well, you got your way." She pressed up against me, and we started to dance very slowly. "I can feel every part of you." I said.

She smiled and said, "Not every part."

"You're gorgeous. What a body!" I said.

"Dave, kiss me again. And hold me tight. You make me feel so safe and secure."

My mind was wandering. Suddenly, after eighteen months of total celibacy, I was holding a beautiful girl in my arms, alone in her bedroom. It was all happening so fast.

She pulled away from me a bit, and began to walk over toward her bed. "Let's lie down," she said, "and let me take your clothes off."

She began to peel off her tight green dress and I tried hard not to lose my cool. With every piece of clothing she removed—from me and from herself—I grew more and more excited. "I love touching you, Debbie," I told her, running my hands over her body. Her skin was so soft, and her curves were gorgeous.

"Dave," she said breathlessly, "do you want to go all the way?"

Boy, did I want to. I kissed her slowly and softly, but then, something started to feel…just not right. I sat up.

"What's wrong?" Debbie asked.

"You're so beautiful, Debbie," I said, "but our first time together should be romantic and meaningful, not slam-bam, thank you, ma'am!"

I looked at her—she was so beautiful, I could hardly believe my hesitation.

"I don't know if I'll ever see you again, Dave," she said, and she looked as though she might cry.

"Of course you will, Debbie." I told her.

But I really wasn't sure. There was two hundred miles between Olean and the Bronx, and I didn't want a long-distance relationship.

The fact that every time I looked at her beautiful body, I kept seeing Irena lying on that stretcher, very still, her white dress turning the color of blood.

"I'm so sorry," I said. "There's…there's more I want to tell you, but I just can't right now."

"What do you mean?" Debbie asked.

"I mean there are parts of my past you don't know, really horrible parts, and they make it hard for me to truly enjoy this moment."

"It's not you," I assured her. "It's not you at all. You're beautiful and sweet. I like you a lot. Like I said, I've liked you all summer. But getting close to someone…" I said, "Is really hard for me."

"I understand." She said.

"You do?" I said.

She nodded. "I do, Dave. I don't know what's happened to you in your past, but I know what it's like to be hurt."

She had my full attention. I couldn't help but be curious about her own history.

"Did you have a boyfriend in high school?"

Debbie's face darkened a little. "I went steady with a boy during my sophomore and junior years," she began. "He was a year older than me. We were very close...we really did everything together. My parents thought he and I would get married after we finished school, and I guess I did, too."

"He graduated last year and went off to Cape Cod to get us a place to live for the summer. We were going to work there. I planned on joining him a little later. But then...just before I was going to meet up with him...I got a letter in the mail. He told me not to come, that he needed some time to think. He said he felt trapped and wanted some space. He said he loved me, but was confused."

I reached out and held Debbie's hand. She gave me a grateful smile.

"I was heartbroken—and angry," she continued. "I was ready to go to Cape Cod, to see him face to face and demand an explanation. But my dad stopped me. My ex stayed there for the summer then left for Boston College. When he came home for Christmas, we had a long talk. He said he'd always love me, but it was definitely over between us."

"Oh, Debbie," I said, holding her close. "What a creep. That guy didn't know what he gave up. You probably had a dozen guys beating down your door."

She shook her head. "A lot of guys asked me to the senior prom, but I turned them all down and stayed home. I haven't gone on a date since I was dumped. I still get angry and sad. Sometimes it's hard to stop thinking about the past, you know? Even if there's something really great in the present."

Wow, even though our situations were very different, she couldn't have said it any better I thought.

"Debbie," I said, "I'm really sorry you had to go through all that. I know exactly how much it hurts to lose someone."

"Did you get dumped, too?"

"Well, not exactly." I said. "It's a story for another time, okay?"

She nodded. "Okay. I won't push you to talk about it. You can tell me when you feel like it." She laid her head on my shoulder.

"You know I would never want to hurt you," I said softly.

"I know. I feel very safe with you." She said.

"Maybe you shouldn't, Debbie."

"What do you mean?" She asked.

I stroked her hair. How could I tell her I'd only been with one girl—and that girl was dead?

"It's hard for me to talk about it," I said.

"Okay." She was so sweet and unquestioning. I was beginning to fall in love with her.

"I really like you, Dave," she said, as she began buttoning her blouse. "I'm glad we didn't go all the way. The truth is that I would like to get to know you better. Who knows if that's going to happen, since you're headed back home. But you never know what the future holds."

"You're right, Debbie. Who knows what could happen?"

I kissed her on the forehead as we prepared to say our goodbyes.

"Can I have a kiss?" I asked.

She gave me a devilish grin, then laid one on me that made my head start to spin all over again.

"So long, Debbie," I said, and felt a strange sensation in my heart when I realized it might be the last time we ever saw each other.

"So long, Dave," she said, and gave me a look of such intensity I thought it would burn right through me. "Let's not say goodbye, okay?

"Okay," I agreed. "We will see each other again and soon."

Vince Romanelli slipped an envelope across the desk.

"It's all there." Vince said.

Even in the dark of the office, Vince noticed a greedy glint in Fletch's eyes as he reached for the envelope.

"What'd you find?" he asked.

"Plenty." Vince answered.

Fletch rubbed his hands together. "You, my friend, are a prince among paupers. And a talent among fools."

"I do my best." Romanelli couldn't suppress his smile. He knew he was damn good at what he did—the best in New York, as a matter of fact. That's why he could charge a pretty penny for his services.

Victory Night

Fletch shook out the envelope as a stack of papers and photographs fell onto his desk. He sifted through the documents. He didn't know exactly what he was looking for, but he knew he had what he wanted.

Then his eyes fell on a photograph that looked like it was taken at a crime scene. Though the photo was black and white, one thing was obvious, a girl had been shot to death.

And there, in the corner of the photograph, was Dave Roth, being held up by a policeman.

"Is this who I think it is?" Fletch asked.

Vince nodded. "It's all there. The newspaper spread, the police report. You've got everything you need."

"You've done well." Fletch said.

Fletch pushed a thick envelope across the desk.

"Consider this your just reward," Fletch said.

Romanelli nodded. He grabbed the envelope and, as quickly as he came, he disappeared.

Fletch reached for one of his finest cigars and poured himself a fresh glass of scotch as he pored over the papers in front of him. The room filled quickly with thick, dark smoke.

"Tonight you had your victory, Dave," he murmured. "It won't be long before I have mine."

CHAPTER 9

Home, Sweet Home

Wednesday morning, I was up at seven and made the rounds to wake up my roommates.

The bus for New York City was leaving at ten, and I didn't want us to be late.

"How do you feel?" Candle asked as we packed.

"Sore," I replied. "That Hare got me good." I pulled up my shirt to look over my shoulder in the mirror. Hare's fastball hit me directly on my knife wound. The skin around the thin white line was deep purple. The scar didn't bother me much these days, but then I usually didn't get hit by a baseball going at least ninety miles an hour. The steady flow of beers had numbed the pain the other night, but today, two days later, it hurt like hell.

Candle agreed. "It's an ugly wound."

"Dave!" I turned around to see Aunt May, the wonderful seventy-year-old widow who had generously shared her rooming house with us that summer, standing in the doorway. "Your mother and father are on the phone, dear."

"Thanks, Aunt May." I went downstairs to the kitchen where she kept the phone.

"Congratulations, Duv!" boomed my Dad's voice. He always addressed me as Duv, Yiddish for Dave. "We're proud of you."

"Thanks," I said. "Thanks for calling. I'm sorry we missed each other yesterday."

"You know how much we wanted to be there," Mom said.

"It's okay," I said. "I'm so happy to hear from you both. This phone call makes the victory complete."

"We tried to call last night," my mother said, "but we couldn't get through."

"We love you, honey," my Mom said.

"I love you, too," I said, trying not to get choked up. After everything I put my parents through, they had every right to disown me and never speak to me again. Instead, they were calling to say how proud they were of me.

"Well," I said, clearing my throat. "The bus leaves soon, so I should probably get going."

"Okay, Duv, we look forward to seeing you soon" my Dad said..

"We're glad you're coming home," my Mom chimed in.

"Me, too." I swallowed hard. "And I've got some exciting news to tell you when I see you. You're not going to believe it. See you very soon, okay?"

As I hung up the phone, I wondered if what I'd just said was true. Was I happy to be coming home? I wasn't sure. The only thing I was sure of, was seeing Mom and Dad.

By eight, we all made our way outside and waited on the stoop with our suitcases, feeling sad. It wasn't easy saying goodbye to Aunt May, who was so good to us all summer. Every one of us had genuinely come to love her. Before we left, she gave us a beautiful red tin filled with her homemade chocolate chip cookies.

Leaving the rooming house was one of the strangest feelings I ever had. It didn't feel real. I felt numb. I had so many great memories of this place. Yes, the South Bronx was home...but what was "home,'" anyway? There were darker parts of my life that had never crossed the Hudson. Here, in Olean, I'd been given a new chance at life. As a result, my memories are pure.

Maybe that makes it a fairy tale, said a dark voice in my subconscious. In your heart, will you always be a warlord from the South Bronx? Were these last few months even real?

A dark cloud settled over me again, and I couldn't shake my gut feeling that a storm was brewing.

It was almost time to go—but not before my last meal in Olean. I tried to quiet my troubled mind as we walked into town one last time.

❖ ❖ ❖

The diner was packed. Most of the team was there, plus fans, fans, and more fans. Candle, C, and I got a table in the back that they reserved for us, but I couldn't eat much, the numbness and anxiety had turned into an empty, sick stomach. The other guys, it seemed, felt the same.

After half an hour, I said, "Guys, let's take a long, slow walk to the ballpark," and they all agreed. We reminisced as we walked, and each of us had a story to tell—every one of them heartwarming.

When we got to the clubhouse parking lot, our team bus that had Yankee pinstripes all over it, was waiting for us. There was also a big crowd of fans, friends, and a handful of reporters. I saw Sandy Abrams in the crowd.

"Dave!" Sandy called out. "How do you feel about being called up to the Major Leagues—the New York Yankees, no less?"

"We're all excited about going to New York and working out with the Yankees," I replied. "Especially about playing them in the exhibition game on Saturday."

She excitedly shook her head, her long blonde hair framing her face. "That's not what I meant," she said. "I mean how do you feel about being on the roster and pitching against the Red Sox next week?"

My teammates turned to look at me.

"Is it true, Dave?" Candle asked. He looked hurt that I didn't tell him this before.

I nodded sheepishly.

"It's true. I just found out the other night, I didn't want to take anything away from our team celebration."

For a moment, I was afraid my teammates would be jealous or resentful. But I should have known them better than that.

"Let's hear three cheers for Senor Dave!" Candle shouted, and suddenly the entire team and everyone who had gathered to say goodbye erupted into spontaneous cheering. I felt humbled and loved.

After a few minutes of congratulatory hugs and handshakes, Sandy pulled me aside from the crowd.

Home, Sweet Home

"You realize, Dave, now that you're going to THE SHOW, you're a shoe-in for a *Look* cover story."

"Wow," was all I could say.

"I'll be in touch with you over the next couple of days," Sandy said. "I'm headed back to the City, too—classes start again tomorrow. Let's plan for a lunch date."

"Great." I paused. "Do you need my number?"

"Oh, I've got it." She gave me a sly smile. "I'll be seeing you Dave," she said, as she turned around, flipped her hair off her shoulders, and walked back into the crowd as I admired her.

A moment later, Mayor Martinson arrived to bid us all farewell. He asked the fans to make a line so they could each say their goodbyes to us. It was happy and sad all at once. We signed a ton of autographs, took pictures, shook hands, and hugged almost everyone. I kept scanning the audience for one person in particular, and finally, I saw her.

Debbie was standing on the outskirts of the crowd with her brother Alexander. She was wearing a tight sweater and a short skirt, and looking absolutely stunning. I went over to give her a big warm hug. I told her how beautiful she looked.

"Thank you, Dave," she whispered back, her eyes shining.

I thanked them for coming to see the team off, then reminded Alexander to focus on being a good person first, and a good ballplayer second.

"You'll be back, right Dave?" he asked.

I looked at his big sister, and something passed between us

"Alexander," I said, patting him on the head. "we're friends for life. This is only a 'so long,' I promise. I'll come visit you, or you'll come to the Bronx…" I looked at Debbie. That last line was meant for her.

"Would you come to the Bronx?" I said, soft enough that Alexander couldn't hear.

"If I'm invited," she replied, a sparkle in her eye.

"Then consider yourself invited." I leaned in and gave her a kiss on the cheek. I wanted it to be more, but Alexander was watching.

"See you soon, Dave," Debbie said, as she took Alexander's hand.

I stood on the bus steps and looked at the crowd one last time.

Feeling emotional, I gave them a big wave. "So long, everyone. I'll never forget you!" I yelled with tears in my eyes.

"So long, Dave!" they cried.

Suddenly overwhelmed, I climbed quickly onto the bus and sank into a seat. I closed my eyes as I heard the door shut behind me.

CHAPTER 10

Back In The Bronx

On the bus, they gave us sandwiches, and we had all kinds of cookies we got from our fans. We were all very excited about going to the Bronx and meeting the Yankees.

At that point, eating kosher was pretty much out the window for me. I'd started the summer trying to eat solely from the kosher section of the Olean Deli, but you could only eat kosher salami for so long. I felt guilty, but justified it with the fact I said my prayers faithfully every day.

After the sandwiches, we opened up the red tin of Aunt May's homemade cookies, and they were gone before you could say "chocolate chip."

We were stuffed by the time Shultzy came around to hand out our meal money for the few days in the Bronx—$50 in fives. He also gave out copies of our schedule. Our estimated arrival time at the Concourse Plaza Hotel was 2:00 p.m. I asked Candle if he wanted to come with me to my old neighborhood when we got there.

"Si, si," he responded.

"Great," I said. "The schedule says we have to be in the lobby at seven for a team meeting, then dinner in the main dining room at seven-thirty. That should give us enough time to say hello to my Mom and Dad and tell them the good news."

I knew Candle came from an upper class family in Venezuela, so I wondered what he would think of my family, my neighborhood.

"You sure you want to come?" I asked.

"Why?" he asked, looking at me quizzically. "Shouldn't I?"

"Well, it's the South Bronx. Sometimes it's not pretty."

Candle put a hand on my shoulder firmly. "I'm with you all the way, my brother."

"Thanks." I felt good about going back to my neighborhood with Candle, a friend from my new life, by my side.

"We'll take the trolley," I said. "I bet you've never been on one?"

"No," Candle said, "Never."

He closed his eyes and rested his head against the window, and before I knew it, he was asleep, just like almost everyone else on the bus. The sandwiches and chocolate chip cookies had worked better than a sleeping pill—everyone was out like a light. The few guys who weren't snoring were staring out the window, lost in thought. This was a very different road trip than any other we had taken all season.

I couldn't sleep, so I took out my diary and started writing. It was a habit I picked up in jail, writing in my diary every day, reflecting on my life and the world around me. It was one of the only things that kept me grounded.

I must have been writing for a couple of hours when the bus pulled over to a gas station on Route 17 in Kiamesha Lake, New York, in the heart of the Catskill Mountains. I completely lost track of time. We all got out of the bus to stretch our legs and hit the john. I took a big, deep breath. The Catskills is a wonderful resort area in upstate New York. It just smelled so good.

Once we were back on the bus, everyone seemed to be in higher spirits. As we got closer to the Bronx, no one could sleep anymore. When we went over the George Washington Bridge, I started playing tour guide and directed the driver to the Concourse Plaza Hotel, pointing out some landmarks to my teammates along the way: Fordham Road, the Loews Paradise Theatre balcony, and Ripley's, the legendary men's clothing store where I got my Bar Mitzvah suit, as did generations of Bronx boys before me. I gave them some colorful personal anecdotes about each place, and they were eating it up. I was, too—being the tour guide was fun.

We got to the hotel just before two. As we got off the bus, we all looked around like a bunch of tourist kids in a candy store. There was a banner hanging over the front entrance that read:

WELCOME TO THE TEAM OF DESTINY

We all just stood there and stared at it like we'd never heard the phrase before.

"Soldiers," Skip said, moving us back into action. "Let's go check in."

"Yes, sir!" a bunch of us called out in response.

The lobby looked like a cathedral, but we didn't have a lot of time to stop and look around. Our suitcases were brought in and we got the keys to our rooms. Skip and Shultzy went with the team bus to the stadium and dropped off our gear while the rest of us went to our rooms.

"Look at this place," I said to Candle. Both of us were in awe. "It's huge. I was never in a hotel lobby like this before."

As soon as we could, Candle and I headed out of the hotel and walked over to East 149th Street and the Concourse to catch a trolley. It was a beautiful day for a walk, the City was starting to cool down after a steamy summer day. To my surprise, I realized I was enjoying being back home in the Bronx.

As we walked, I pointed out some more landmarks—the Bronx County courthouse, Cardinal Hayes High School, the main Bronx post office. Finally, we reached East 149th Street, paid our five cents each, and boarded a trolley.

"There's Modell's," I said to Candle, pointing out the window. "That's where I bought my sports equipment. And there's—"

Suddenly, there it was, stretching endlessly, green outside the trolley car like a ghost, St. Mary's Park. I couldn't finish my sentence. The memories of that night came crashing over me like a tidal wave.

"Dave?" Candle looked at me with concern. "Dave, are you alright?"

"I need to sit down." I answered.

He helped me to one of the shiny trolley seats as my legs gave out.

"Was that where it happened?" Candle knew enough of the story to piece together what we just saw.

"That's it," I said, barely above a whisper.

"It must be hard, seeing it now." He said.

I shook my head. "I didn't think it would affect me this much. I thought it was all behind me, but I guess not."

"It may be behind you," Candle said wisely, "but that doesn't mean it still isn't hard."

Candle was so wise, it never ceased to amaze me. He seemed much older than his nineteen years.

"And there's the church," I said in a dull monotone. St. Rock's Cathedral looked so large outside the window. "That's where she was headed that night. She was going to mass." Candle was also Catholic, and I knew he appreciated the ironic tragedy of Irena being killed on the way to mass, where I had no doubt she planned to pray for our safety.

"Are the gangs still at war?" he asked quietly, as though he didn't want anyone to hear.

"I'm sure they are, Candle," I said. "It never ends."

We sat in silence a long while until finally, we reached Prospect and Southern Boulevard, where we got off.

We walked a couple blocks to my street and, as we got closer, I felt a strange feeling in my stomach. I didn't know how I would be treated. My guys may have resented that I left the gang life, especially now that I had experienced some success. Maybe they didn't want me to come back, and I wasn't sure I wanted to be back.

Candle couldn't stop looking around wherever we went, obviously overwhelmed with the size of the buildings and how crowded everything was. The cobblestone streets and trolleys had his total attention.

"Dave," he said, watching a trolley roll by, "the streets are beautiful."

I nodded. I guess they were if you never saw cobblestone streets before.

We walked by the Ace Theatre, where I used to go to the movies. *Frankenstein* and *The Return of the Wolfman* were playing. Then we passed Auggie's, where I used to play pool and hang with the guys.

"Hey, there's one of my guys," I said, noticing a familiar character coming out of Auggie's. "Richie!" I called, and he turned toward me.

For a moment, I wasn't sure what he would do. Riccardo Corda, who everybody called Richie, was one of my closest friends in the Wildcats, a loyal gang member and an even more, loyal friend. He was a couple years younger than me and I helped him stay out of trouble many times. Was he angry that I'd left the gang and then the Bronx, abandoning all the guys?

My question was answered the moment I saw a big grin spread across his face.

"Hey, Davey!" he said as Candle and I approached. "How da heck are ya?"

"Good. You?" I asked.

"Give me a hug, man, we missed you!" Richie said, grabbing me roughly.

"I missed you, too." When I was able to step back, I added, "Say hello to my roommate, Candle."

He gave Candle an appraising look. I realized that, since Candle was dark-skinned, Richie may have thought I was hanging out with a rival gang member—one of the Puerto Ricans, even.

But then Richie turned back to me with a funny look. "You gone queer?"

"Don't be a wise guy," I said, and Richie laughed. "We were roomies during the season. Now be nice and don't tick me off."

"Okay, Davey, just testing to see if you went soft on us." He held out a hand for Candle to shake. "Hi, Candlestick, gimme five." Candle shook his hand and smiled, though I was sure that Richie had thrown him for a loop.

"Richie, where are the boys?" I asked.

"Probably at Portnoy's, working, or in school. Today's the first day back—the end of summer stinks, big time!"

"Did you go to school today?"

"No way, man! I didn't feel like it! Davey, we got a big money stickball game at six, and sure could use you. The Rockets are coming up from Spanish Harlem—and they're good."

Hearing the word "Rockets" sent a chill down my spine. I hadn't heard it in a long time.

"Alejandro?" I stammered.

"Nah, man. No one's seen him since the rumble. He did a little jail time, then split town. Nobody's heard nothin' from him. You're safe, Davey Boy."

I coughed. "Wish I could play, Richie," I said, "but we have to be back for a team meeting at seven. Sorry."

"Yeah, man!" was all Richie had to say to that. "See ya, Davey," he added as he began to walk away, but then turned back. "Listen, we're all happy for you, man. You got out."

The guys were happy for me. That meant a lot—more than I could say.

"Thanks, Richie," I called after him. "Tell the guys I said hi and I'll see 'em soon."

He waved to me over his head and kept on walking.

"Wow, Dave," said Candle. "I think your friends respect you quite a bit."

"They're good guys," I said, and meant it. "They all got a rough start on life. But they would have my back in an instant—I've never doubted that. I wish there was some way I could show them that there's more to life than gang wars, stickball, and hanging out at the corner candy store."

"You are showing them that, Dave," Candle said, putting his hand on my shoulder. "You showed them that by having an amazing season in Olean, and you're going to show them that even more next week when you pitch for the New York Yankees."

I thought about it for a moment, then smiled. "You know what, Candle? You may be right." I grinned. "And you know what? 'Cuz you're so smart, I'm going to treat you to an egg cream."

"A what?" Candle asked.

I laughed, then took Candle straight to Portnoy's candy store where I promptly bought him an egg cream. Egg creams are a Bronx and Brooklyn specialty, a drink that has neither egg nor cream, instead they're made with chocolate syrup, milk, and seltzer. And not just any chocolate syrup but Fox's U-Bet Syrup...or it's not a genuine egg cream.

Candle had never had one before and seemed a little put off by the name, but as soon as he tried it, he loved it.

When we were done, we continued our journey through the neighborhood.

We passed the Hires Root Beer factory, where I worked from time to time, during the summers. There was P.S. 62, my old elementary school. Seeing the schoolyard brought back a lot of memories. I played a lot of basketball, stickball and softball games there. It was also our gang meeting place.

Finally, we got to my apartment building, 660 Southern Boulevard. "Candle, let's say hello to Mom and Dad."

I hope they're home. I knocked and knocked, but no one answered. They must not be home from work yet. I was anxious to share the news about pitching for the Yankees, and eager for them to meet Candle.

Unfortunately, I didn't have a key, so I couldn't show Candle our apartment. A flood of nostalgia came over me as I looked at the apartment door number, 1D, which was our home all my life. It was small but impeccably clean and tastefully furnished. Mom and Dad came to America through Ellis Island from Kiev, Russia in the Ukraine, and Warsaw, Poland. They worked very hard for everything they achieved. I knew they were proud of their home, and as their son, I was proud of it, too.

I slipped a note under the door, telling them I would call them later. We checked our watches and realized we better start heading back to the hotel.

On the way, we stopped into Bernie's Luncheonette. Bernie Allen was one of my good buddies, I worked for him part-time all through high school. He was happy to see me and as funny as usual—Bernie was also a stand-up comic, and did gigs on weekends. He gave us buttered Danishes and egg creams, which Candle and I happily accepted. Bernie eventually went on to Vegas and became a star!

We decided to take a taxi back to the hotel so we wouldn't be late for our meeting.

As I stepped into the street to hail a cab, I saw a familiar face across the street. My heart froze in my chest. It was Connor O'Neill, Big Joe's brother.

"Davey!" he shouted over the traffic. "Hey Davey, wait up!"

Candle saw my reaction and asked, in a low voice, "Dave, who is that?"

"It's Big Joe's younger brother," I said stiffly.

I stood still as Connor ran across the street, wondering what I would say to him. I wasn't sure there was anything to say. Connor was never with the Wildcats—he was too young at the time. From the little I knew of him, he was an okay kid. Despite Big Joe and Connor's father's drunken rages, the youngest O'Neill had turned out alright. Word on the street was that he was a good student who had his head on straight. But in that moment, I could only think of Connor as Big Joe's kid brother. That blood bond blocked everything else in my mind.

"Davey," Connor said finally, as he stood beside me on the sidewalk. "Long time no see, brother."

The word "brother" sent a chill down my spine.

"Long time," I said.

I sized Connor up. He had filled out a good deal in the last year; he was bigger and older looking. He also looked tougher. I wondered how he was doing in the wake of Big Joe's disappearance.

"How's school?" I said, trying to think of a neutral conversation.

He stared at me. "Screw school," he said. "School's for brown-nosers."

I was very surprised by his attitude, until I remembered that Connor wasn't a kid anymore.

"They can't teach me crap," Connor frowned. "At least not the kind of stuff I need to know to get by."

"We heard you're headed to the big leagues," Connor said. "Pitching for the Yankees next week, against the Red Sox. Nice work."

"Thanks," I said, pleased that the guys were keeping up with my baseball career.

"Who's the spic?" Connor said, gesturing toward Candle with a shrug.

I felt Candle tense up beside me. My instinct was to punch Connor in the face for a comment like that. But the last thing I wanted to do was stir up trouble on my first day back in my neighborhood.

"He's with me," I said. "My teammate and roommate. And one of the finest ballplayers you'll ever see and my friend."

That shut Connor up.

We stood staring at each other in silence. It was obvious that there was much to say, but neither of us wanted to say it. I wondered if he would bring Big Joe up.

"Well, we've got a team meeting to get to," I said firmly.

"Yeah, I've got to meet the rest of the guys at the schoolyard anyway."

I raised my eyebrows. "You got a rumble tonight?"

Connor laughed. "Nah. Just a stickball game this time. But I figured we could use a little practice, so I called a meeting."

"You called a meeting?" I was confused.

"Yeah." He stared at me. "Didn't you know? You're looking at the Wildcats warlord."

The news bowled me over. After I got out of jail, I'd made a clean break and cut ties with the Wildcats completely. But I still kept up with the guys that I considered my friends. Something like Big Joe O'Neill's younger brother taking over the gang seemed newsworthy.

I wondered why Richie hadn't told me about Connor taking over the gang when I saw him earlier. Maybe he was afraid I would be angry. If so, he was right, I was angry.

"Since when have you been a Wildcat, Connor?" I said, trying to keep my voice level.

"I joined the gang a few months ago," he said. "I've been warlord for a couple of weeks."

So it was a recent development, that's why I hadn't gotten word of it.

"The Rockets still giving you trouble?" I asked.

Connor growled. "If that low-life wetback Alejandro shows his face around here again, we'll give him more trouble than he can handle."

Amazing, I thought, how a few months of gang life on the streets can turn even the nicest kids into hot-headed, rabble-rousing bigots. I shook my head.

"Well I wish you the best of luck," I said, deciding it was best for me not to get into it. "From a former warlord to a present one, don't let the job get to you. It can be an awful lot of pressure on just one guy."

Connor shrugged. "I haven't had any problems yet." He was looking me straight in the eye, like he wanted to pick a fight.

"We'll have to finish this conversation later," I said. "We have to go."

With that I grabbed Candle's arm and directed him toward the taxi, while Connor stood with his arms folded, staring at us as we left.

CHAPTER 11
Trouble Brewing

Candle and I sat very quietly in the back of the taxi as I looked out the window, seeing scenes from my street life fly by.

"Dave," Candle asked after a while, "why does everyone call you 'Davey'?"

"That's what I'm called in the streets," I replied. "It's a show of affection, I guess. Everyone gets a 'y' or an 'ie' at the end of their name. Like Richard is called Richie."

Candle thought for a moment and said, "Richie seems like a nice guy."

"He is" I said. "But he shouldn't be skipping school. Someday, I'll tell you more about the streets of the Bronx."

We rode in silence for a while, then Candle spoke. "It's interesting. The street life is all about affection and friendship...but it's also about fighting and killing."

"Kind of crazy?" I said.

"Very," Candle said, obviously lost in thought. "Do all the gangs have weapons?"

"Well, I actually tried very hard to keep our rumbles weapon-free. Heck, I tried to avoid rumbles all together. I wanted the guys to play sports instead, like stickball, but sadly, zip guns won out, like the kind Big Joe had with him that fatal night."

"What's a 'zip gun'?" Candle asked.

"It's a homemade handgun that shoots a .22 bullet."

"That doesn't sound friendly at all," he said, looking upset.

"It's not," I agreed.

Back at the hotel, Candle and I went to our room to unpack and get dressed before our team meeting. I took a moment to say my prayers.

The phone rang at six-thirty. It was my folks, calling to say they were sorry they missed us. They were looking forward to seeing me and meeting Candle tomorrow. I told them about my good news. I could hear them crying. I told them I would tell them more about it, when I saw them tomorrow. When I hung up, I thanked God that I had a Mom and Dad who loved me so much. I was all they had left. My younger sister Esther died from leukemia at nine-years-old. Understandably, they never got over it – and neither have I.

As I got dressed to go downstairs for our meeting, Candle sat on the edge of his bed, thinking.

"What's on your mind, Candle?" I finally asked. "You look like you're in a whole other world."

"I guess I am, Dave," he said. "This is all so strange to me."

"I know, I told you about my past life when we were in Olean…but it must be crazy to see it all in real life and real time." I said.

Candle nodded. "Yes. Now that I know where you came from…I respect you even more for everything you've accomplished."

"Thanks, Candle. I appreciate that a lot, coming from you. "

We finished unpacking, and got dressed to go downstairs for our team meeting.

The sun was setting over Yankee Stadium as a tall, white-haired man made his way up the stairs to Fletch's office. He was dressed in a smart three-piece pinstriped suit. The way he held his hat in his hands gave him the air of a distinguished gentleman. He tapped lightly on Fletch's door.

"Come in," Fletch said in a rough voice.

"Tobias," Fletch said. "Good to see you."

"The pleasure is mine," Tobias said.

"Please, sit down." Fletch motioned him to a chair. "Can I offer you a cigar?"

"What are you smoking these days?" Tobias asked.

Trouble Brewing

"Only the best for you, my friend." The GM turned to the glass case behind him, surveying his extensive collection of fine cigars. He picked a La Meridiana Kohinoor, a Tabacalera Cubana. They were the most expensive cigars sold in the United States, each packaged in its own wooden "coffin."

Fletch opened the box and took a cigar out. Then he opened a cabinet and pulled out a black cigar cutter. He clipped the cigar, lit it with a match, and handed it to his guest.

"Scotch?" Fletch asked.

"Brandy, please."

Once they each had a drink in hand, the two men settled into their chairs.

"How's business, Toby?"

"Not bad. Could be better. They don't make journalists like they used to."

"I could say the same for some ballplayers." Fletch responded.

Tobias recollected the last time he was in Fletch's office—three years earlier, when he was running a cover story on Jackie Robinson. Fletch had used some choice words in describing Robinson. Toby couldn't determine whether the GM was more angry that the baseball legend was playing for the Dodgers, or that a black player had broken the color barrier in the Major Leagues.

Fletch exhaled. "We've got some injuries to our starters this year. Not the perfect time, while we're in a heated race for the American League pennant."

"And you've got a big game with the Red Sox coming up," Tobias said, puffing on his cigar. "The whole world's going to be tuning in, especially with Ted Williams back from Korea. We just did a feature cover story on him last week."

Fletch's face dropped. "I know. I read it."

"Public sympathy for the Red Sox is strong, Fletch. They're getting a lot of attention with Ted's return." Tobias said.

"My owner and manager have suggested we take drastic measures to stir up the pot." Fletch laughed. "I can't say I agree." Tobias responded, "They may be right. If you want to take the stage, you have to pull a coup to get the limelight off of Williams right now."

"How about a scandal involving a Yankee player?" Fletch said casually.

"What kind of scandal? A marital affair? " Tobias asked sarcastically sipping his brandy…"That's not news."

"What about murder?" Fletch countered.

Tobias sat up a little straighter in his chair. "Now, you might have something."

"We're pulling up a player from our Minor League team in Olean, New York." Fletch said. "He was the PONY League MVP, the Olean golden boy. He's scheduled to pitch for us against the Red Sox next week. That game could potentially be our pennant clincher."

Tobias raised his eyebrows. "Pretty big game to be trying out new talent, don't you think?"

"Believe me, it wasn't my idea. But Casey and Mac are all for it. They think it's our only option." Fletch responded.

"And how is murder in the mix?" Tobias asked.

Fletch tapped his finger on the rim of his glass. "Turns out the player's background is far from spotless. He was a gang warlord in the South Bronx. He was involved in a sticky situation with the leader of a rival gang and the guy's pretty young cousin."

"Sleeping with the enemy?" Tobias said.

"You got it." Fletch said. "Turns out the kid was heavily involved with the girl. But something went sour during a rumble, and she got shot."

"Did your guy do it?" Tobias asked.

"Jury's still out on that one." Fletch responded. "He served time in the county jail. His father bailed him out. He went back to Morris High School to finish his senior year. The circumstances are murky, but his name is far from clean."

Tobias looked thoughtful. "Bad press," he said.

"Exactly." Fletch rubbed his hands together. "There needs to be more of it."

"What are you asking, Fletch?" Tobias asked.

Fletch took a sip of his scotch and just stared at Tobias.

Finally Fletch said, "I know about your bid for mayor, Toby," staring at Tobias. "What a pity that your campaign for councilman wasn't successful. For what it's worth, I think you would make a fine mayor. I'd be happy to help out in any way I can. As it turns out, I know people in pretty high places. Powerful people, too." Fletch continued.

Tobias met his host's stare by staring back. After more than forty years in the journalism business, he could read people effortlessly. He knew all about human nature, especially the darker side of it. It didn't take a rocket scientist to understand what Fletch was asking…and what he was threatening if he didn't get what he wanted.

"You want the cover?" Tobias asked, his voice steady.

"Yes. Feature cover story." Fletch said. "Pull out all the stops. Did you have anything better scheduled?"

"Only an Eisenhower feature," Tobias replied. "But we've already done two in the last three years. I think we can push it back. We were planning to give the Yankees a little ink, anyway, with the World Series imminent. We had another story in development, as a matter of fact. So we'll just move it up."

"Excellent." Fletch said.

The men sat in silence for a moment, reflecting on the deal they just made.

"Who's the player?" Tobias asked finally.

"Dave Roth."

A flash of recognition passed over Toby's face. Fletch caught it.

"You know him?" Fletch asked.

"Heard of him, yes. My…one of my sports reporters was telling me about him just yesterday. She was thinking of doing a story." Tobias said.

Fletch responded, "Perfect. Now she'll get her chance."

Fletch reached into his desk drawer and took out the envelope Romanelli had given him.

"I think you'll find everything you need in here, police write-up, photographs from the crime scene, the long and short history of David Roth."

Tobias hesitated a moment, uncertain whether or not to touch the envelope. He pressed his lips together, picked it up, and tucked it under his arm.

"It's always a pleasure to see you, Tobias. It's been far too long. By the way, you can plan on my total support for your mayoral campaign, just let me know what you need." Fletch offered.

"Agreed." Tobias stood up, brushed the ashes off his suit and said "Thank you for supplying *Look* magazine with…a provocative story. It's sure to draw some attention, and we do enjoy publishing pieces that get people talking."

"It's what I call good journalism. The people get a good story, the Yankees get rid of a bad seed. And you, my friend, get an exposé that will rock the world of Major League baseball." Fletch said.

"What more could anyone want?" There was a sarcastic tone in Tobias' voice that did not go undetected by Fletch.

"I'll say one thing about you Jews," Fletch said, flashing a satisfying smile as Tobias put his hand on the doorknob. "You know a good deal when you see one."

"Yes, we Jews do," Tobias said.

And with that, Tobias Abrams, the President and Publisher of *Look* magazine, walked out the door.

Tobias thought to himself…With a name like David Roth, he's probably Jewish. Is this really about his past troubles, or is about him being Jewish?

CHAPTER 12

Sandy Abrams

The team met up in the lobby of the hotel and went to a conference room for a meeting.

"Listen up, men!" Skip said as soon as we sat down. "Please say hello to Tom Rizzo, the Yankees publicity director."

There was a loud roar, a hoot, hoot, hoot from all the guys.

"Thank you for that fine welcome," Mr. Rizzo said. "I also want to welcome you to the Bronx. The Yankees are very proud of what you've accomplished this season. The Team of Destiny is getting a lot of well-deserved press, so it's important that I remind you what your Uniform Players' Contract says, to help with our protocol."

Rocky raised his hand, "Mr. Rizzo?" he asked. "What's protocol?" As usual, he never failed to make everyone laugh. Rocky was great at loosening us up.

Even Mr. Rizzo was smiling. "Your name?" he asked.

"Rocky Tunina."

"Rocky, protocol is the proper procedure to use, if a member of the press wants to do a story or you're asked to do a product endorsement. Please refer them to me for clearance. If the Yankees front office approves, we'll notify you immediately. If you don't hear from us, forget it! Any other questions?" There was silence. "As a specific example, Dave, the President of *Look* magazine called to get permission to do a feature on you. How do you feel about that?" Mr. Rizzo asked.

I was a little embarrassed to be singled out like that, but happy Sandy had come through. "Flattered," I replied. "But the feature should be about our team, not just me."

"Should I tell him no?"

"It's your shot to call, Mr. Rizzo. I'll do whatever is good for the Yankees."

"Thanks, Dave. We'll move forward with the feature on you then. It'll be good publicity and a morale booster for the entire Minor League system. It'll also encourage other young ballplayers to sign with the Yankees. Please remember, guys, I'm with the Yankees all the time, home and away, and I'm always here for you. Skip?" he concluded, turning the lead back over to him.

"We'll leave for the stadium tomorrow at 1:55 sharp," Skip said. "Don't forget your jackets and ties. Your gear is already in the clubhouse. Each of you will be sharing a locker with one of the Yankees."

There was a loud roar, and more hooting.

"Listen up!" Skip shouted, trying to calm us down. "Shultzy will explain the rest."

Shultzy moved in front of us. "Tomorrow, when we get to the clubhouse entrance, police security may ask your names and code. Our code is **champs**." He paused for more hootin'.

"When you get in, bear left and follow the signs to the executive offices. There will be people waiting there to give you your plane tickets home. On their desks will be letters of the alphabet, indicating where you should go according to your last name. For example, Rocky, you'd go to the table that says 'S–Z.'"

"Shultzy, I understand," Rocky said. "It's protocol!"

We were all hysterical again.

When we settled down, Shultzy said, "After you get your tickets for Sunday—"

Another roar went up—hoot, hoot, hoot!

"—you'll be taken to the clubhouse to suit up for batting practice. See the clubhouse managers for your unies and further instructions. And now, boys, enjoy dinner on the New York Yankees!"

We all headed to the main dining room, where there were chandeliers and big, round tables covered with white tablecloths. The banner that had been on the front of the hotel earlier was now hanging in the dining room.

Wow, I thought. Now we're in the big leagues!

"Look at this place!" I said to C and Candle. Their eyes were as big as mine.

"I've never eaten on a white tablecloth," C said in awe. "Not in all my life."

"Me, neither," I confessed.

We stuffed ourselves with shrimp cocktail and filet mignon. And when the free wine started flowing, we were truly in heaven.

"I could get used to this," Candle said.

"Me, too." I said.

After dinner, I was so full that I planned to go right upstairs to bed. But then Rocky had an idea.

"Let's go absorb a little local color!" he said.

We decided to go have a beer at a local pub. Why not? It had been a long day of travel, and we figured we all deserved to lay back and unwind.

A few of the older players begged off and went back to their rooms, but the rest of us walked outside and found a beer and shot joint down the street. We walked inside and I couldn't help but notice the dingy decor and the attractive waitresses. It made me think of Debbie. I imagined her working the late shift, and the way her legs looked in the white socks she wore to work. I suddenly missed her very much.

"Ready to celebrate New York Style?" Rocky said with a big grin.

"Yeah, man!" I replied. The other guys cheered.

"First round's on me," Rocky offered, pulling out the fifty bucks Shultzy gave us.

An hour later, everyone bought a round. We were pretty far gone, singing, carousing and carrying on. A couple of guys had broken off from the group to go play darts. Someone whispered something about having to keep curfew, but the other guys shut him up.

"We're only young once!" Rocky said, raising his mug of beer. "And you guys are young and single!" He was joined by a round of "Damn straights!" and "Amens!"

Dean, the pretty boy among us, moved over to a petite brunette sitting at the bar. It wasn't long before they were slow-dancing in the corner. A few other couples were scattered around dancing, too.

"Wish I had someone to cozy up to," C said.

"Yo tambien," Candle said, who often reverted back to Spanish when he was drinking.

I found myself thinking about Debbie's gorgeous body, and how nice it would be to have her here to dance with.

"Hey, slugger."

There, standing in front of me, was Sandy Abrams. She was wearing a form-fitting pink blouse that dipped deep enough to reveal a good part of her cleavage. Her leather skirt hugged her curves in all the right places. This outfit was a long shot from the professional reporter clothes she was wearing when we met in Olean. I was speechless. She looked so hot I wasn't sure what to say.

"Sandy," I managed to get out. "You look great."

"I clean up alright," she said with a grin. "You don't look so bad yourself."

"Guess I clean up alright, too."

I tried to keep thinking about Debbie, but it was damn near impossible when there was a beautiful blonde standing two feet away from me who was as sexy as hell.

"You come here often?" Sandy said with a smirk.

"Very funny." I said. "This must be your hangout since it's so close to Columbia?"

She shrugged. "Well, tonight I just happened to be in the neighborhood, so I thought I would drop by and see if any of my friends were here."

I noticed how full Sandy's lips were, they were a deep shade of red. I also noticed she was more dressed up than anyone else in the bar.

"Care for a dance?" she said. "Don't worry—I won't let it affect our professional relationship." She gave me an inviting smile.

"Well, in that case, what have I got to lose?"

Sandy grabbed my hand and led me out to the makeshift dance floor. The music had changed to something a little more upbeat, so we did the Lindy. Sandy was a great dancer, though it didn't take me long to realize she was pretty looped.

After we danced for a while, she wanted to take a break. We made our way back to the bar.

"Can I get you a beer?" I asked.

She shook her head. "I only drink hard liquor. I'll take a double scotch on the rocks."

I was a little surprised at what she ordered. She obviously knows her way around a bar.

As she sipped her scotch and I finished my beer, I asked her where she was earlier.

"I was at a birthday party for one of my friends," she explained. "Then my father called about something kind of important. Looks like we got clearance for the *Look* feature and cover."

She smiled, but there was something I couldn't quite place behind her eyes. I didn't like the look of it. You're reading too much into it, I told myself. It's late and you're tired.

"That's great," I said. "I never doubted you."

"It's coming out sooner than we thought, too."

"Really?" I said.

"Yeah. It's going to press by the weekend."

"Holy cow." I was surprised. "Great news from the lady reporter." I said.

She responded quickly, "I don't see a lady here."

I couldn't decide if her forwardness was charming or distasteful.

"I might as well ask you some questions right now," she said, pulling her notepad out of her purse, "since my dad's going to kick my butt with this last-minute deadline."

"Okay," I shrugged. "Whatever works for you. Be careful, we both had a lot to drink."

Sandy and I sat very close to each other for the next half hour as she asked me questions about my past, present, and future. We talked about my baseball career, my personal heroes, my aspirations. When it was time to talk about my history, I didn't mention my gang relationships, and she didn't ask.

After another round of drinks, Sandy and I were sitting even closer together and slurring our words a little bit. Every time she leaned forward to write something down, I got a lovely look down the front of her blouse.

"Well, I think that's enough questions for tonight. Looks like I have all I need." Sandy said, as she put her notepad back in her purse. She smelled incredible, her perfume had a spicy aroma, like cinnamon. I knew one thing for sure, Sandy was hot!

"Sandy," I said slowly, trying desperately to keep my wits about me. "It's late. Can I walk you back to your dorm room?"

"Oh, I don't stay in the dorms," she said. "I have my own apartment."

My heart stood still for a moment.

"But sure," she added coyly, "you can accompany me there if you would like."

I said goodbye to Candle, who was very tipsy. "I'll either be back here later or see you at the hotel," I told him. I pointed to the unfinished beer in front of him. "Go slow."

"You go slow, too," he smiled lazily, eyeing Sandy.

"Let's go, Sandy," I said, leading her out of the bar.

I put my arm out and she held on tightly. She was a little wobbly, but we made it with no major incidents. She gave me her key and we took the elevator up to her apartment.

Once we got there, she let me help her out of her jacket, then I put her to bed.

"Dave, come here," she said as I fixed the blanket around her. "Can I kiss you?"

"Sure," I said, leaning in. The minute our lips touched, it was like fireworks exploded. It was a very sexy kiss.

"Want to make love?" she asked.

Did I ever! But I needed to clear my head.

"Not now," I said, using all my willpower. "Maybe another time though, okay? Sleep tight, Sandy." I kissed her on the forehead. "Goodnight."

I stood outside Sandy's apartment for a full minute, wondering what the heck was wrong with me. A bright, beautiful girl wanted to have sex with me and I turned her down? It just didn't seem right to take advantage of her when she was clearly bombed.

I caught a cab back to the bar, where Candle and C were having a drunken conversation on race. Dean had disappeared with the pretty brunette, and the other guys had stumbled back to the hotel. The joint was nearly empty. I sat down next to Candle and ordered another beer. We talked for a while, about life and baseball, then C said he was turning in for the night. When he was gone, Candle asked me about Sandy.

"You like that girl?" he asked me, his accent stronger than ever after a night of booze.

"Sure," I said, though in reality I was not sure what I felt for Sandy. "I'm not ready for a relationship."

Candle nodded. "I understand. At home, I met a wonderful señorita, too…Maria Rivera. I had to decide on my career and college, or marriage. I chose to follow my feelings—to play baseball and become a doctor, like my father and mother. Maria and I believe there is always time for commitment…and I believe the later the better."

We both laughed. Then Candle continued, "When dos people are secure with themselves, they can live a happier life together. Dave, can I give you some brotherly advice?"

"Yes, por favor."

"You have a great career in baseball and you must get your college education. Focus on those goals. You will be muy successful. Commitment can come later. For now you might as well have a good time."

I slapped him on the back. "You know what, Candle? My night just got a whole lot better, thanks to you."

He winked at me as I threw some coins on the counter to pay for our drinks.

"Where are you headed, my friend?"

"To have a good time," I said with a grin.

The next thing I knew, I was knocking on Sandy's apartment door. "Dave," Sandy said when she opened it. "I'm glad you came back.

Thanks for taking such good care of me." She giggled. "I was a little drunk." From the way she wobbled a little bit while standing, I could tell she still was.

"Me, too," I admitted. "Feeling better now?"

She asked, "How much better?"

"Oh, much." I said.

Suddenly, her lips were all over my neck as she kissed me. She grabbed at my shirt buttons.

"Damn, you're aggressive!" I said.

She stopped. "Too aggressive for you?"

"Hardly," I said.

"Mmm." Sandy stroked my chest, sending chills down my spine. "It certainly seems like you've had some experience. I wasn't expecting someone so young to be so exciting."

"I've been around the block."

"High school girlfriend?" she asked sweetly.

I turned onto my side. "Yeah. Something like that."

"Lucky girl," she said.

"No," I said, bitterly. "Unlucky girl."

"Oh, Dave," Sandy sighed, her breath warm in my ear. "It wasn't your fault."

I froze.

"What wasn't my fault?"

Sandy suddenly sobered up. "I just mean...what happened to your girlfriend...you can't blame yourself."

I turned around and looked at her.

"How do you know? You don't know anything about it. Do you?" I searched her face for clues, but she wouldn't look me in the eye. "Do you, Sandy?"

"I...I don't know what you're talking about," she stammered.

"Is this all a part of the interview?" I said, raising my voice.

She looked a little scared. "I don't know what you mean, Dave," she said.

"Well you don't know me," I said. "You don't know me at all. And don't pretend to."

"I know you a lot better than you think, Dave Roth," she said quietly.

"Oh yeah?" I said, as I shoved my feet into my shoes and walked toward the door. "We'll see about that."

CHAPTER 13

The Yankee Stadium

"Duv, Duv, wake up! Duv!"

It was my Dad. What was he doing in my room anyway? "Hi, Dad" I said. The beers from last night were not out of my system yet. Then I remembered my night with Sandy and how it ended, not so good. "Is everything okay, Dad? Is Mom okay?" I asked. I jumped out of bed and gave him a big hug.

He kissed me and said, "All is well. You just overslept. I met your roommate Roman downstairs and he gave me the key to your room. He said it would be nice if I surprised you."

"Good to see you, Duv," he said.

"You too, Dad." I wondered why Candle didn't wake me up. My father looked confused. "Candle is our nickname for Roman," I explained.

"I imagine he was a little surprised himself. He had a big surprise this morning too—his whole family is here! They arrived from Venezuela, their flight landed at Idlewild in the middle of the night." Dad told me.

"Wow," was all I could say. That was bigger than big!

"Mom is waiting downstairs," Dad said. "I'll let you get ready. I couldn't wait to tell you how proud of you we are."

"Thanks, Dad" I said. "Let me get washed up and I'll see you downstairs, okay?"

Dad left and I got ready, but first, I said a quick prayer to thank God for Candle's blessings.

After washing up and getting dressed, I went downstairs. Mom and Dad were waiting for me in the hotel lobby.

"Oh, Duv," Mom said, her eyes filling with tears. "You look so good and handsome. I'm so happy to see you!"

I hugged her for a very long time.

"Good to see you too, Mom. I missed you a lot this summer."

"We missed you, too, honey, but we couldn't be happier for you." Mom said. "What a wonderful summer you had!" She smiled proudly…while tears streamed down her beautiful face. "Our son, THE BALLPLAYER!"

"Things are looking up for the Roths," I said. "I want you both to be proud of me. No more gangs."

"Oh, honey," Mom said, cupping my face in her hands. "No matter what happens, we are always proud of you."

"Shall we eat?" Dad said.

"Sure, Dad," I said with a big smile as we went into the dining room.

"Dave!" Candle called out when he saw us. He came over and shook my hand excitedly and then took Mom, Dad and me to meet his entire family—his father, Albert; mother, Joanna; brother, Felix; sisters, Roseanna and Alicia, and girlfriend, Maria Rivera. Candle introduced me me as his "other brother" and Mom and Dad as his extended family.

I hugged them all, still not believing they were here. "I'm totally overwhelmed," I said. "It's a pleasure to meet everyone. I feel like you're my family, too!"

We all had breakfast together, and talked, and talked, and talked. The Vilchezes were a wonderful family and we got along famously. How lucky I was, I thought, to have two families.

"Hey Candle," I said. "How would you and your family like to come out for beer and pizza to one of my old local hangouts, after the game this afternoon, in my neighborhood?"

Candle thought for a moment. "No one's going to insult my family, are they, Dave?"

I shook my head, "Absolutely not. If they do, they'll have to deal with me."

"Okay," Candle said. "In that case, we're in."

THE BALLPLAYER

Later that morning, as Candle and I got ready to catch the team bus to the stadium, I told him how much I liked his family. I could tell my Mom and Dad liked them, too—they had volunteered to take the Vilchezes around New York sightseeing while Candle and I went to work out with the Yankees.

Candle said he was glad we all got along so well. He asked if his brother could move into the hotel room with me, so that he could have the other room with Maria. How could I refuse?

I made a concerted effort to focus on baseball for the next few hours, and pushed Sandy to the back of my mind. Candle and I were looking good in our jackets, white shirts, and ties. All the other guys looked great, too, very polished and professional.

We drove to the stadium in our pinstriped team bus that our fans had covered with huge signs announcing we were the PONY League Champion Olean Yankees, people on the streets were waving and car horns were honking. Photographers and press were all over the place. If anyone hadn't heard of the Olean Yankees before, they sure knew who we were now!

Our bus stopped in the parking lot in front of the players' entrance. I couldn't believe the huge crowd waiting for us there, yelling our names and asking for autographs. And this was only a practice session for us!

It took the team almost half an hour to work our way to the clubhouse door, the security police had to line up and make a path for us to get there. I went directly to the clubhouse since I wasn't going home on Sunday and didn't need to pick up plane tickets like the rest of the guys.

Inside, I finally met up with Little Pete, the clubhouse manager. He was a short, likable guy who immediately made me feel welcome. He put a hand on my shoulder. "Welcome to the New York Yankees," he said.

"It's a dream," I said, looking around the locker room.

"Dave, you're sharing this locker with Eddie Lopat," he told me with a huge smile, pointing toward a locker nearby. "He requested it."

I didn't know what to say—what an honor! I hadn't seen my friend and mentor in many months.

Pete told me how everything worked. "Every roster player is required to sign forty-eight baseballs every home game for the concession stands. He led me to another room, a lounge full of sofas, where players could relax, watch television, read newspapers, and look at any new announcements on the bulletin board.

Next came the trainers' room, the showers and, as Pete called it, "Casey's office."

Seeing us outside the door, Casey came out to say hello.

"Dave Roth, Mr. Stengel," said Little Pete.

"We met in Olean," Mr. Stengel said, shaking my hand.

"Yes, sir." I responded.

"Well, it's good to see you here. Welcome aboard." Casey said.

Pete led me back to the locker as he gave me the rest of my instructions. "Your unie and sanies are in your locker. Workout starts in fifteen. While you're out there signing autographs is okay—in fact, it's encouraged by the Yankees. There'll be plenty of fans in the stands, even though it's just a general workout. That's how committed they are to the game. If there aren't any questions, I'll see you later."

"Hey, Pete," I said, grabbing him before he ran off. "One question. We're going to Tony's 149th Street Bar for beer and pizza later today. Wanna come? It's in my neighborhood."

Pete grinned. "Sure, sounds like fun."

Just then, I saw Eddie Lopat come into the clubhouse.

"Mr. Lopat!" I stammered.

"Dave," he said, coming over to shake my hand. "I heard about your start! Welcome to the big leagues!"

"Thank you. I owe it all to you, Mr. Lopat."

"Not hardly. You had the talent and were a great student. You really listened, learned and worked hard." He smiled and put a hand on my shoulder. "I knew you would get here, I just didn't think it would be this quick!"

"Thank you, Mr. Lopat." I said.

"Please, call me Eddie," he insisted. "We're teammates now. Best you get suited up!" He goosed me and grinned before heading out to the field. I just stared at him—teammates with Eddie Lopat? Was I dreaming?

I quickly finished changing into my uniform then followed him outside. In the runway from the clubhouse to the dugout, Eddie introduced me to Hank Bauer.

"Pleased to meet you, Mr. Bauer!"

"That's Hank to you, my boy. We're teammates."

"Yes, sir!" I said.

In the dugout, I came upon Phil Rizzuto, the Yankees shortstop, who asked, "How you doing, Dave?"

"Mr. Rizzuto, I'm fine. Floating on a cloud." I couldn't believe he knew my name!

"I'll bet," he said, shaking my hand. "Please, call me Phil. We're all so proud of you—you'll make a terrific addition to an already great team."

"Thanks, Phil. I must be dreaming. Could my life change this fast?" I responded.

He smiled at me, as if he knew how I felt. "It can and has—but don't *you* change!" he said.

It was a beautiful day. Standing in the dugout, looking up at the field and stadium, everything seemed perfect and the grass was so green, even the brown dirt looked edible. The scoreboard was unbelievably huge. I was on this field dozens of times for my early morning practices with Eddie Lopat, but it had never looked like this before. Suddenly, growing up in the South Bronx, gang life, Irena's murder—it all faded away. And right then, I had a glimmer of what pure happiness must feel like.

I went out to the mound, just to stand on it. Eddie Lopat came out to join me.

"Hey, Dave?" he said.

"Yes, Mr. Lo—Eddie?"

"Where are your shoes?" he asked.

"I left them in the dugout." I answered.

He laughed. "Why?"

"The field is so perfect, I don't want to mess it up." I said.

The Yankee Stadium

He patted me on the shoulder, still laughing. "It's okay. We've got a pretty good grounds crew. Go put your spikes on."

By the time I headed back to the dugout and retrieved my shoes, most of the players were warming up. The Yankees were out on the field as batting practice started, and all of us guys from Olean were standing around in a daze. I went to the outfield and shagged some fly balls, but it was tough to concentrate with so many stars around—Mickey Mantle, Yogi Berra, Phil Rizzuto, Whitey Ford, Johnny Sain. I thought, what a pitching staff the Yankees had! I couldn't believe I was about to be one of them. I noticed that Vic Raschi and Allie Reynolds were absent, and then I remembered that was the whole reason I was there in the first place.

During the workout, Yankee announcer Mel Allen approached me and asked if we could go to the bullpen for a brief interview. Of course I said yes.

When we got there, he set up the interview by saying, "How about that?" into his microphone. "Ladies and gentlemen, I'm here with Dave Roth, the wonder boy who won the Olean Yankees their PONY League championship game. Dave, how does it feel to be in the big leagues with the New York Yankees?"

"Well, Mr. Allen," I began, "I'm no wonder boy. I grew up in the South Bronx, so to answer your question, this is a dream! I'm thrilled beyond words—that's how it feels. And I sure didn't win the championship game alone…I couldn't have done it without the rest of the Olean Yankees, the Team of Destiny!"

"Thanks, Dave. I'm sure we'll be seeing a lot of each other!" he said.

I shook his hand. He seemed like a nice guy. "You're welcome, Mr. Allen."

I headed back to the dugout, itching to play some baseball. "Rocky," I said. "I want to throw a few. Would you please catch me?"

"You got it!" he said.

We found a spot along the right-field box seats. As I started to warm up, a small crowd formed by the railings. Some of the Yankees were looking on as well.

I was feeling pretty loose. "Rocky," I said, "I'm going to air out a few."

"You got it!" he yelled.

Bang, bang, bang. My fastballs were jumping and made a big, beautiful sound when they hit Rocky's mitt. The noise even got Mr. Stengel's attention—maybe that was my intention all along.

Casey Stengel himself came over to see what all the fuss was about. Skip said, "Dave, what are you doing?"

"I haven't thrown in a couple of days, Skip. I thought loosening up would be good."

"Let him throw a few more!" Casey said. "This kid can throw!"

"Okay," Skip said. "Whatever you say, boss."

Bang!

"Holy cow," Casey said again. "That must have been over a hundred. Hey, kid, show me what else you got!"

I let Rocky know what to expect, then threw two curveballs, two changes, and a fastball.

"Great stuff, kid," Casey said. "That's enough for now. Save it!"

I nodded, smiled at Rocky, then ran out to right field to do some wind sprints. I did twenty, working up a sweat and feeling great. On the way back to the dugout, I saw a little boy in the stands waving his Yankee program over his head.

"Hey, mister!" he yelled.

"Me?" I said, not sure if he was talking to me.

"Yeah, you!" He looked up at me with a big smile. "Sign my program?"

I was surprised but honored. In a second, I gave him my autograph.

"Thanks!" he called over his shoulder as he ran back to where his dad was sitting. "You're the best, Dave Roth!" he yelled.

A big smile spread across my face. This was all too good to be true.

"Dave! Dave!"

I turned to see Sandy Abrams rushing down the steps in the stands.

"Dave, listen, I need to talk to you. It's really important."

I studied her for a moment, and shook my head.

"Sandy, I really don't..."

She cut me off..."I've been at the *Look* offices all morning. The issue comes out tomorrow. You're the cover story..."

This time, I cut her off.

"Sandy. I really appreciate you doing the feature— But right now, I need to focus." I started to turn around, and stopped. "Look, I'm sorry for the way we left things last night."

She shook her head. "It doesn't matter, Dave. You don't owe me an apology. But I may owe you one very soon."

I had to admit, I was curious. But this wasn't the time or place. I needed to be with the guys out on the field.

"I'll talk to you later, okay, Sandy? Thanks again for a memorable night." I said.

"But Dave..." she stammered.

She looked troubled. For a moment, I thought she was about to cry.

"Okay," she said, defeated. "But for what it's worth: I'm sorry. I'm really sorry."

I wondered what she could possibly have meant.

CHAPTER 14

Back In The Neighborhood

As our team bus pulled up in front of Tony's 149th Street Bar, I wondered how many of my Wildcat buddies would be there. Tony's was our favorite hang-out, they have great apizza, cold draft, and a super juke box. Sometimes the crowd at Tony's could get a little rough. I hope not today.

I must have talked up the place pretty good, because everybody came. There was Candle's family, my folks, and all of the Olean Yankee players. Skip and Shultzy tagged along, so did Little Pete and Eddie Lopat, who followed the bus in their own cars.

As soon as we stepped into Tony's, the familiar surroundings made me smile. There was a long wooden bar on the left, some tables on the right; a little further back, up four steps, there was an eating area roped off for us—literally—with a big, homemade sign hanging from the rope that read, "Reserved Strictly for the Olean Yankees and Our Davey."

I got Mom, Dad, and the Vilchezes settled at some tables. Tony thought of everything—there were already two pitchers of cold beer, bottles of soda, and two large apizzas on every table, plus another long table full of apizzas for us. I inhaled two slices in a heartbeat. It was just as I remembered. Tony's mom ran his kitchen and made the apizza using her homemade sauce, fresh mozzarella cheese, sliced tomatoes, oil, and basil. It was better than a kosher hot dog. Well, a little better.

Just as I was about to make some rounds and socialize, my buddy Richie came up and asked me to have a beer with him.

"My pleasure," I said. "First, let me introduce you to some people." I brought him around the tables to meet Skip, Eddie, and Candle's brother, Felix. Richie welcomed my teammates to the neighborhood, and offered them a drink on the Wildcats, and asked Candle and Felix if they wanted to join our gang!

The offer made me a little uneasy, but Candle accepted it right away. He smiled broadly and said, "Yeah, man!"

That was the perfect answer, and we all had a good laugh. It broke the tension.

Richie and I got a couple of beers and sat down in the corner to catch up.

"So when were you going to tell me that Connor was the warlord of the Wildcats?" I asked.

"Yeah, man," he replied uneasily. "Sorry about that. Guess it slipped my mind when I saw you yesterday."

Judging by the way Richie was avoiding eye contact, I'm sure it was not an oversight.

"He's a better guy than Big Joe was," Richie went on. "For one thing, he's not as mean. He's been a good leader so far. I know he's got our backs."

"That's good," I said to Richie. "I'm glad it's working out." I wondered if Richie felt like I still had his back. I may have been out of the gang, but I didn't want to throw my friendships down the drain. I grew up with these guys, and I'm feeling like they think I abandoned them.

I finished my beer in one gulp and excused myself to circulate with Candle and Felix, promising Richie I would see him later. I wanted to talk to as many people as I could. Everyone seemed to be having a good time. A lot of my teammates went over to say hi to my folks and the Vilchezes. The rest of them ate, drank, and talked. It was a great party, and I was happy I put it together.

As I headed back to my table to sit with my folks, I suddenly noticed it had become very quiet. I saw the reason everyone was so quiet. Standing in the doorway with both fists clenched, was Alejandro. He was wearing his red bandana, the Rockets' gang color, and looked like he was ready for a fight.

"Dave," Candle said in a low whisper, "Is that who I think it is? Is that...Irena's cousin?"

"Yes, Candle," I said, "It is."

I knew immediately what I needed to do. I walked right over to him. "Alejandro," I said. "Let's take this outside."

"Screw that," Alejandro replied spitting on the floor by my feet. "If I want to talk here, we talk here."

Suddenly, I felt Richie and Connor move up behind me, putting up a wall. I felt the blood rush to my ears, just like it used to before a rumble. Not good, I told myself. Take it easy.

"What are you doing on our turf?" Connor asked. "Thought you left town."

"Guess I'm back," Alejandro said with a sneer. He turned to me and said, "I hear you're a hotshot Yankee ballplayer now."

Richie answered for me. "He's pitching for da Yankees next week. What's it mean to you?"

Alejandro barked. "It doesn't. Our justice system sucks. They let a criminal out of jail to play in the big leagues."

A whisper went through the crowd. I was burning up. Alejandro had no right to bring up my past in front of my friends and family, most of whom had no idea what he was talking about. I searched the crowd for Tony, who was standing behind the counter ready for action.

"That's enough," I said, staring at him. "This is something between you and me, Alejandro. If you want to talk to me man to man, fine. But I don't want to fight you."

Alejandro looked like he wanted to rip the skin off my face. I could see his anger rising.

"We have a score to settle, Roth," Alejandro said. The veins in his neck were popping. "You and I are not finished." He turned to the rest of the group. "I hope you all know that you're cheering for a phony and a killer."

Mom and Dad were shocked and Candle's family looked horrified. A lot of the guys on my team were staring at me in bewilderment. I was speechless—I didn't know what to say.

"If it's a fight you're looking for," Connor said, stepping out in front of me, "then it's a fight you'll get. But it won't be against Dave. It'll be against the Wildcats." He turned to me and put a hand on my shoulder, "Once a brother, always a brother."

I didn't know what to say. I looked at Connor, Richie and Alejandro, then back at Candle, Skip, Shultzy, Eddie, and the rest of the Olean team. Some of them looked like they wanted to stick up for me, but they didn't know the rules so they were standing awkwardly on the sidelines. It was like my past and present lives were facing off, and I was being pulled in two completely different directions.

Suddenly, Alejandro turned toward the Vilchezes. He said something to them in Spanish, then shook his head. They looked too surprised to respond. Now I was really angry.

"What did you say to my friends?" I said, my blood boiling.

"I said they probably do best to part ways with you. The longer they stick around, the more they're headed for real trouble." He said again. "I thought you'd learned your lesson, Roth. We don't mix white with brown."

Candle walked over to me and put a shaky hand on my arm.

"Hermano a hermano," he said. He looked at Alejandro defiantly. "Dave is my brother."

Alejandro yelled angrily, "That's what you think. He'll stab you in the back too." He gave me a fierce stare. I thought of the irony of this statement, considering it was Alejandro who stabbed me in the back the night of the rumble.

"I'm not the same person I was," I said quietly, hoping there was still some way I could save face. "What can I tell you that could make any sense to explain why she was taken from us? It was a senseless tragedy."

"You're right," Alejandro nodded. "It was senseless. And you were responsible for it. That means there's blood on your hands."

I shook my head, not wanting to believe it. He pointed at me.

"Don't think you're special, you're a piece of crap, and abused my cousin" he said. "I know who you are, and I know where you belong. Right here in the Bronx, in an alley with my shiv in your back."

The crowd was so silent you could have heard a pin drop. Finally, Connor spoke.

"Why don't you head back to Spanish Harlem, Alejandro? I think it's time you left before I put a shiv in your back."

Connor lost his patience and lunged toward Alejandro, but Richie pulled him back. Alejandro swiftly sidestepped the attack. I could feel everyone around me holding their breath, fully aware that a major fight could break out at any minute.

Alejandro glared at me as he walked out the door and said, "You're going to pay, man."

People began to leave. A few of them came up to me, stumbling over their excuses, others didn't even say goodbye. Eddie, Skip, and Shultzy left without saying anything. I couldn't blame them—they were probably shocked, and too decent to embarrass me.

The Vilchezes seemed very nervous. They said they wanted to go back to their hotel room. They begged Candle to come with them, but he said no, "I will stay with Dave". I felt lucky to have such a loyal friend, but I felt very guilty that I put everyone in danger.

After a while, it was just Candle, Richie, Connor and me. Mom, Dad, and the Vilchezes, with the rest of the Olean Yankees took the bus back to the hotel. We sat around in depressed silence, drinking one last beer as Tony wiped down the bar.

"I'm sorry I couldn't call the cops or nothin'," Tony told me apologetically. "I don't screw around with the Rockets. They started a brawl once that knocked out my front windows and wrecked the bar. It almost put me out of business. Besides that, they bashed a guy's head in."

"It's okay, Tony," I said, and meant it.

Connor was eager to talk revenge. A move like Alejandro made—not only coming onto our turf, but insulting a former Wildcats warlord—was unprecedented. It was a huge slap in the face, and no way was Connor going to let the gang pride go unprotected. He had challenged our honor, and the only way to protect it was to fight. This was the gang code.

"I'm talking bats, shivs, zips—the whole shebang," Connor said excitedly. I realized that this would be Connor's first rumble since becoming warlord, which is why he was envisioning a blaze of glory.

"I don't want to fight, Connor." I said. "I've seen rumbles. I've led them. And they aren't pretty. I don't want anyone getting hurt."

"But he insulted you, Dave!" Connor protested. "He insulted us."

"I know that. I don't like it, either. But I'm not the same guy I used to be. I'm not in the gang anymore and I don't want to be. I'm also not guilty of anything I was charged with. It's like I was guilty before proven innocent. I've got a game to play next week. Fighting isn't going to solve anything." I can't believe I said all that…man have I changed.

Connor laughed bitterly. "You've been out of the South Bronx for, what, one summer? How quickly we forget."

He chugged the rest of his beer and slapped Richie on the back.

"C'mon, Richie," Connor said. "Let's go find someone who's not a deserter. We'll go somewhere where our friendship is wanted."

Richie gave me a sad look, finished his beer in one gulp and left.

"I'm sorry, Davey," he said. "But we're not playing by da same rules anymore."

"Beat it, guys," Tony said.

"We'll be seeing you," Connor said angrily.

"Bye, Davey," Richie said.

Candle and I were left to finish our beers in silence. I wanted to tell him how much I appreciated his friendship, even when there was nothing to say. But I couldn't find the words. Instead, I apologized.

"I'm so sorry your family had to see this," I said. "It's not at all how I imagined the day would be."

"It's okay." he said. "What will you tell them, about all the things Alejandro said?" I asked.

"The truth" Candle said. "As long as that's okay with you."

"Yes, your family deserves to know the truth." Dave said.

"Doesn't everybody?" Candle asked.

"Maybe. But not yet. I feel like I'm so close…"

"You don't want to ruin it for yourself?" Candle finished my thought.

"Yeah." I paused. "Is that wrong?" I asked.

Candle said, "Everyone has a past that haunts them, Dave. You must choose whether or not to let yours control your future and life. It's your choice."

I nodded, absorbing what he said.

We settled up with Tony, and apologized for the way the day turned out.

"Some party," I said, as we were leaving.

Candle did his best to give me an encouraging smile. "Tomorrow's a new day, mi amigo."

CHAPTER 15

Bad Press

The next morning—I got up at five and took a cab to the 92nd Street Y. I was in desperate need of a good, long swim.

I loved to swim ever since I learned how to at Boy Scout Camp Ranoquow, where I went for two weeks when I was twelve. For me, it was a way to get focused, meditate, and de-stress. Swimming, praying, and keeping a journal were the best remedies I knew for quieting a troubled mind.

But that morning, swimming didn't have its usual calming effect. I stayed in the water for almost two hours, doing lap after lap, trying to forget what Alejandro had said. Maybe it would just blow over and things could go back to how they were over the summer, when life was golden and I didn't have to focus on anything but baseball.

What bothered me the most was that deep down, I feared he was right. I knew I didn't kill Irena, but as the warlord, I should have made sure Big Joe never took that gun to the rumble. I should have protected Irena better. Alejandro was right, there was blood on my hands.

Back at the hotel, I had just enough time to shower, dress, and get to the dining room by ten.

"Good morning," Skip said when we were all in our seats. "I'm sure you all agree that last night was...different. I just want to say one thing about that, and then no one needs to bring it up again. We all have things in our past that we probably don't want to talk about. Dave's just happened to be a warlord of a gang in a tough neighborhood. We know he's a great teammate and a stand-up guy, so let's all be there for him."

"So, men—let the past be the past and focus on what's ahead. We have a fun day ahead of us. When we take the field for our workout at twelve, some of you will shadow the regular position players. For example, Rocky, you'll follow Yogi. When he takes BP, just be there—don't get in his way. If he tells you to hit, you hit. If not, forget it. Just watch and learn, okay?"

"Skip?" Rocky asked from the back of the room. "Do I shadow Yogi everywhere he goes, or only on the field?"

God bless Rocky, I thought, as we all broke out in laughter. Leave it to him to shake us out of our gloom and doom by being his usual self.

"I think it's best to limit your shadowing to the field and dugout," Skip replied. "Let the man pee in peace. Bobby, you shadow Martin. Dean, Rizzuto. Candle, you got McDougald, C, Mantle. Rippili, Bauer. Pitchers and everyone else, shag balls and hang with the players in the outfield. Dave, you're not to throw today."

"Stengel wants you to hit when Lopat hits. Skip also told us Lopat is starting today."

We got on the bus promptly at eleven, and on the way to the stadium, Skip gave us a pep talk.

"You guys earned every minute of this dream trip—and, soldiers, it is a trip! Tomorrow, we'll show them why we're the Team of Destiny. Now, let's go have some fun playing baseball in Yankee Stadium."

Again, there was a huge crowd waiting for us at the clubhouse entrance, and we signed lots of autographs and took pictures, as we inched our way toward the players' entrance.

"Dave! Dave Roth!" I turned to see a reporter with thick glasses scribbling furiously on a pad of paper. "What's your response to the allegations, Dave?"

Suddenly, all the other reporters were pressing in tightly around him. They were shouting questions and trying to get my attention. Everyone was talking at once.

"Can you refute the evidence?"

"How does Yankees management feel about this?"

"Did they know the truth when they signed you, Dave?"

"How do you know this 'Sandra Abrams'? Former girlfriend? Jilted ex?"

The onslaught was so dizzying, I could hardly make out a single question. I caught words here and there. *Allegations…evidence… truth…Abrams…*

I had to sit down. I unapologetically pushed through the remaining crowd until I made it inside the clubhouse. Tom Rizzo, the Yankees publicity director, was waiting for me in the hall.

He stared at me a long time before speaking.

"Follow me, Dave," he said firmly. I walked down the corridor to his office. Once we were inside, he closed the door. I had a feeling I was in some serious trouble.

"Take a seat."

I sat down and waited. I didn't have to wait long.

"I suppose you know what the big fuss is about."

I looked at him helplessly. "Actually, sir, to be honest…I have no idea." My mind was still scrambling to fit the pieces together.

Rizzo dropped a copy of *Look* magazine in front of me. It hit the surface of the desk with a loud smack.

"Look familiar?" he asked.

I looked down at the picture on the cover and recognized it instantly. Although the photo was in black and white, my memory filled in the blanks—the green grass under our feet, the red blood on Irena's white dress. And me, collapsed in the corner with Lieutenant Fabrizi holding both of my arms.

"What do you have to say, Dave?" Rizzo asked, his voice even.

I struggled to find an answer. My mind was reeling from this turn of events. Remembering that fateful night was one thing, but having the cover of *Look* magazine in front of me, was to much to take.

"I…I can only say I'm sorry, sir."

"Is it true?"

I swallowed hard. "Yes, it's true."

He gave me a hard look.

"So you killed Irena Rosario."

"*What?*"

He gestured toward the magazine. "Take another look, Dave."

I forced myself to look down again, and this time, my eyes focused on the headline instead of the picture. In big, bold letters, it read,

Newest Bronx Bomber A True Killer.

And the subheading underneath: "Pitcher Roth's Police Record Overshadows Won-Lost Record."

My eyes lingered for just a moment on the byline. Of course I knew what it would say, but that didn't keep my heart from sinking when I saw on the cover, *Sandra Abrams*.

"This isn't what it looks like," I said regaining my voice.

"Really? Then please tell me what it looks like. Because it looks like you were the warlord of one of the most notorious gangs in the Bronx. It looks like you shot your girlfriend one night at a rumble, the girlfriend who also happened to be the cousin of your biggest rival. It looks like you went to jail, then staged a massive cover-up before joining the New York Yankees Minor League team. Or at least, that's what Ms. Abrams would have us believe."

"She's got the basic outline but not the facts," I said.

"Do you know this Abrams girl, Dave?"

"A little. She covered our championship game last week in Olean."

"Have you had a relationship with this girl?"

I looked away. Two days earlier, it would have been easy to answer that question with a flat-out, "No." But now I wasn't sure what to say.

"Not a relationship, sir, not exactly…" I wasn't sure how to finish my sentence.

Rizzo let out a long, exasperated sigh. "Well, frankly, Dave, it doesn't matter. I don't give a damn what your relationship with Sandra Abrams was, is, or ever will be, but I doubt you're headed for the altar after this whopper of a story." Rizzo picked up the magazine and tossed it in his garbage bin. Then he turned and looked at me.

"You're a good kid, Dave," he said. "I see it, Skip sees it, Shultz sees it. The media's good at whipping themselves into a frenzy. Give 'em a bone and they want the whole cow.

I've seen them make messes like this before, and I'm sure this won't be the last." He tapped his fingers on the side of the desk. "I'd like to give you an opportunity right now to tell me what really happened that night. I want your side of the story, unfiltered. I want you to tell me the truth. Can you do that?"

I took a deep breath.

"Yes, sir. I can."

And I did.

❋ ❋ ❋

As I sat in Tom Rizzo's office telling him the real story of what had happened on April 29, 1952, the New York City press machine was operating in overdrive. Everyone who was anyone had gotten wind of the story. *The Post. The Daily News. The Daily Mirror.* The city's tabloids were thrilled to have such a juicy exposé just a couple of weeks before the World Series. Reporters from every paper in New York sank their teeth into this one.

Meanwhile, Sandy Abrams sat angrily in the *Look* office of The President, her father, Tobias Abrams.

"I don't like it, Dad," she said. "It's sensational expose journalism. I thought *Look* was above that sort of thing." She frowned. "I thought *you* were too. I know I certainly am."

Toby sadly said, "I agree. It's not the kind of journalism we like to publish. But I didn't have a choice."

"Really? Sandy asked. Because you always told me the one thing no one can ever take away in life is your ability to choose."

Her father shook his head. "Maybe when you're older, you'll understand."

Sandy rolled her eyes and pushed the magazine away from her. "I'm sick of looking at it. Sick of that lurid headline jumping off the page and that tasteless photograph. I hate that my name is on it. I hate that you made me do it, and I hate whoever it is that made you do it. And don't pretend you don't have ulterior motives for publishing this story."

"Sandy, it's over and done. It's gone to press and we're not going to issue a correction. How about a little gratitude to your old man for getting you a cover story?"

"Oh, the story wrote itself. It didn't matter who wrote it. It might as well have been your secretary for all you care. You just needed a name to stick under that awful headline, and as luck would have it, I was your girl. You knew I was already anxious to do a story about Dave Roth. And you were right. I just didn't think the story would be about a bunch of crap."

"Watch your language, young lady," snapped Abrams. "Now, if you like this boy and you're sorry that your little piece ruined your chances of hooking a husband, then tough luck, kiddo. That's the price of being an investigative journalist."

"That's not it," Sandy said, sounding unsure. "And you don't have to be so mean." She stuck out her lower lip as her eyes filled with tears.

"Look, sweetheart," Tobias said, softening. "If this didn't work out the way you thought it would, I'm sorry. But life's not always fair."

"You know what I think?" Sandy said, her eyes gleaming. "I think Dave Roth was wrongfully accused. He is definitely holding something back—you read his testimony. It was in the stack of papers you gave me. The papers you didn't want me to know where they came from." She looked at her father with a steel gaze, but his face was unreadable. "I don't think he did it," she went on, "and I think the guy who really did it has yet to come forward."

Tobias looked at his pretty young daughter with admiration. No one could argue that she was not smart and determined. He wasn't always proud of his own choices—But Sandy was an upstanding young lady, someone who knew what she believed in and had the guts to say so.

"You know what, Sandy?" Tobias said, leaning toward her.

"What?" She asked.

"You may be right." He said.

Sandy said, "I beg your pardon?" She had heard her father utter those words so rarely in her twenty-one years that she felt she must have heard him wrong.

"I said, you may be right."

"Damn right I am," she said under her breath. She took one last look at the headline and said, "This wasn't how I imagined my first national byline. I'm leaving. Thanks for your time," trying her best to be cordial. "And Dad?"

"Yes, sweetheart?" Tobias said.

"I quit...I won't be writing for *Look* anymore." She savored the look of shock on her father's face. "Thank you for the opportunity to have a cover story. But if we all have choices, then this is mine."

She slammed the door behind her and stomped down the stairs.

❖ ❖ ❖

"Is that it?" Tom Rizzo rapped his knuckles on the desk. "Is that the whole story?"

I nodded. "That's it."

I had told him everything, with the exception of Big Joe O'Neill's name. I confessed that I wasn't the one who brought the gun that night, that someone else had shot Irena and I knew who it was—but I wasn't going to squeal.

"I appreciate you telling me the truth, Dave. Now we just have to figure out what to do with it."

I nodded. "Yes sir. I agree."

Rizzo closed his eyes, deep in thought.

"And no one knows where that guy is?"

"Not that I know of." I paused. "He does have a brother."

"Really? Well, that's a start. Is his brother involved in gang life as well?"

"As a matter of fact...yes."

"Hmm." Rizzo massaged his temples. "Are you on speaking terms with the brother?"

"I was." I answered. "We had a bit of a falling out last night. They want me to come back and fight with the Wildcats against the Rockets. I said **NO**."

"Good," he said briskly. "This *Look* magazine business is a disaster, but it's old news. It happened more than a year ago. If we find a way to clean this up, it's going to be based on the fact that you're not the same kid. You've left that life behind you. Your past is exactly that, your past. But if you pick up with your gang again..." He gave me a severe look. "Then it's all over, Dave. Everything you've worked for, your success with the Yankees so far...it will all be gone in a heartbeat. And we won't be taking you back. Mark my words. Do you understand?"

"I understand, sir."

"Good." Rizzo leaned back in his chair. "Then there's only one thing you can do."

I listened intently, eager for the solution. "What's that?"

"You have to get yourself out of this mess, Dave. If you're firm in not giving the cops the name, then you've got to find a way to get the guy who did it to come forward. You've got to find way to tell the truth and get public sentiment on your side again."

Rizzo pointed to the oversized calendar hanging on the wall. "You're pitching for the New York Yankees in the Red Sox game next week." He said marking his calendar.

I swallowed. "You guys still want me?" Roth asked.

"Hell, of course we want you! You could be one of the best things to happen to Major League baseball since Babe Ruth. You're a good kid with a great future. Now, don't get me wrong. This could completely derail your career...but not if you handle it before it's too late."

"This is still America. innocent until proven guilty, right?" I asked.
"Well, not in the court of public opinion." Rizzo answered. "You've got less than a week to clear your name."

CHAPTER 16

Just A Hunch

I couldn't get myself to join the rest of the guys for their workout. The thought of going out on the field and having to face all those reporters' questions and flashbulbs was just too much. When I found Skip and explained the situation, he said warmly, "Why don't you go home and see your parents. Just be back in time for dinner. You don't want to miss getting your bonus check."

"The Yankees still want to pay me?" I said dejectedly.

"Don't be ridiculous, Dave," Skip said. "Of course they do. They've got to sell you to the public, and I don't know how they're gonna do that unless you can clear your name."

I nodded gratefully, happy for some time alone to clear my head. I took the back entrance so I could avoid the press.

It was all beginning to sink in. I managed to keep my past under wraps for some time. What happened that night in St. Mary's Park, combined with all the stupid choices I made leading up to it, was so painful I had to forget everything.

I hopped on a trolley back to my neighborhood, hoping it would help me figure out how I could clear my name without being a rat.

I decided to go to the shop where my Mom and Dad worked.

As soon as I walked in the door, a few women began to point and whisper. I had a feeling they were talking about me.

"Duv!" my father said. "Are you okay? I thought you were at the stadium working out today."

"That was the plan," I said, "but it kind of changed."

When Mom heard us talking, she came to the front of the shop,

"Hi, darling," she said, giving me a kiss on the cheek. "Everything alright?"

I couldn't tell from their reaction if they had read the article or not. If they had, they were being decent enough not to call attention to it.

"I just wanted to see you both," I said. "I'm sorry I didn't call you more from Olean this summer. I thought of you a lot."

Mom smiled. "It's okay, Duv. We knew you were focused on baseball."

"Duv, are you sure you're alright?" Dad asked.

"I'm okay, Dad. Maybe we can have dinner together like we used to?"

"Of course, honey," Mom said. She gave my arm a squeeze and whispered in my ear. "And don't worry, we know who you really are. You're a good boy and our son. We know you would never hurt Irena, no matter what the papers say."

So they had read it after all. I felt embarrassed but lucky that I had such supportive parents. I thanked them and gave them both a big hug.

Unsure of where else to go, I headed back to Tony's Bar in the hopes that Richie or some of the other guys would be there. I wanted to talk to them about Big Joe. I felt dejected, unsure of where to go and who to turn to, even though it would be easy to clear my name by just giving the police Big Joe Connor's name. But as the ex-warlord, I couldn't do that.

Tony had just opened up for lunch and the place was almost empty. I was grateful for this. It gave me some thinking time.

"Hiya, Davey," Tony said as I came in the front door.

"Hi, Tony."

"We heard the news." He shrugged. "Sounds to me like that *Look* writer got it pretty damn wrong."

"Thanks for the vote of confidence, Tony. I wish the rest of New York City had as much confidence in me as you do."

I ordered a slice of cheese pizza and a Coke. Tony set to work filling the salt shakers while we chatted.

"If there's one thing I can't stand," Tony said, "it's someone so yellow he won't own up to what he did. Look, we all know who really shot Irena that night. You don't gotta say nothin'— it doesn't matter if you sell out or not, 'cuz we all know it was Big Joe."

I sipped my Coke out of a plastic straw and let Tony talk.

"So it gets me angry that Big Joe split town and let you take the heat. And now you've got Alejandro comin' around, trying to stir up trouble all over again. Like one rumble wasn't enough. Like he's gotta spill blood for blood."

I asked Tony, "Do you think Connor was serious last night about declaring a rumble with the Rockets to retaliate for Alejandro's threats?"

Tony shrugged. "Connor talks a big game. He's trying to impress everyone with how big and tough he is. He's the new guy in charge, so he's gotta prove himself, and one of the best ways to do it is to challenge Alejandro."

Just then, Richie walked in the front door.

"Hey, my man," he said to Tony. "Large pepperoni, extra cheese, please. Hey, Davey."

"Hey Rich." I wondered if things would be different between us because of the night before.

"Hear you got some bad press," he said.

"Word travels quick." I answered.

"You're the Bronx's hottest export. What else we gonna do with our spare time other than follow your career?" Rich asked. "I'm sorry it had to blow up like this. It's a load of crap and we all know it. You didn't go near that damn gun." Rich said.

"The Yankees don't know that." I responded. "Maybe I should have told them everything from day one. But I thought it was behind me. I sure didn't think it would come back to bite me in the butt like this." I said.

Richie shook his head and said, "Who's da leak? Sounds like someone got a lot of information and didn't have a problem puttin' you in the crummiest light they could find."

"I told them I honestly don't know. Sandy, that's the girl who wrote it, obviously had connections to someone pretty high up. Half of the pictures in the article I never saw. It looks like they were straight from the police files. Maybe someone on the inside is trying to get me."

"Maybe she's da police chief's daughter or something." Rich said.

Something clicked in my head. "Her dad is the President and Publisher of *Look*."

Richie snorted. "Well that explains da front-page spread."

I barely heard him. The wheels were turning fast and furious in my mind. I didn't trust Sandy farther than I could throw her, but suddenly it seemed like she wasn't the mastermind. Maybe her father had a hatchet to bury. Maybe that's why she had come to the stadium and tried to warn me what was about to happen—she had been strong-armed by her father into doing something she didn't want to do. Who did Mr. Abrams know, and why did they want him to destroy my image? Now if I could just find out where he was getting his information…and why.

"Another slice, Davey?" Tony asked.

I shook my head no. "Where's the closest library?" I asked. Tony and Richie both gave me a blank stare.

"Not exactly top of my list of cool places to hang," Richie said.

"Is that the place with books?" Tony joked. I had to laugh.

"You two jokers," I said, feeling a little more hopeful. "Guess I'll have to find this one on my own."

"Whatcha gonna do there, Davey?" Richie teased. "Find a good looking librarian and whisk her off to the stadium to record your stats?"

"Nah. No more women for me. It's a dangerous game!" I stood up from the bar and stretched. "I think I have an idea who's behind this."

"Really?" Tony looked impressed.

"Not sure of anything yet. It's just a hunch. But I'm going to go find out."

"Well, I had a hunch you'd be playing for da Yankees some day," Richie said. "So looks like hunches have a way of panning out."

I grinned, happy that we were still friends.

"Now get da heck outta here," Richie said. "Or I'm going to go snatch that librarian myself."

The Morrisania Branch of the New York Public Library cast a shadow over McKinley Square in the afternoon sun. I paused for a moment to admire the two-story structure, wondering why I never spent time here before. I asked two policemen and three shop-owners before I could find it. A homeless man on the street corner gave me the right directions.

Inside I piled a stack of newspapers and magazines a foot high. The *Times, Herald Tribune,* the *Mirror,* the *News,* the *Post*—and any other magazine that might have information on Mr. Abrams. Then I realized I was missing one crucial detail, I didn't know his first name. Only one way to remedy that, go straight to the source.

Look didn't seem to be with the other magazines, then I saw it behind the counter.

"Excuse me," I said to the librarian at the reference desk. She was grey-haired with glasses—not exactly the librarian Richie had in mind. "Could I see an issue of *Look*, please?"

"Of course," she said kindly, reaching for the issue with my face on the cover.

"Actually...can you get me any issue but the current one?"

"Alright," she said, reaching underneath for an older issue. From the way she handed it to me, I had a feeling she had just made the connection between me and the picture on the cover.

I flipped to the *Look* masthead and found what I was looking for, Tobias Abrams. Bingo.

From what Sandy had told me, I knew she came from a Jewish family. The conversation I had with Candle at the hotel popped into my mind. It was bad enough that people from differing cultures and religions tried to hurt each other, it was even worse to be attacked by a fellow Jew. There must be a reason, I thought. I never did anything to Mr. Abrams. What did he have against me?

I sat at a long wooden table and began poring through the papers and magazines one by one, looking for any mention of Tobias Abrams that might give me a clue. What charities did he give money to? What were his personal and professional connections? Who was he trying to impress?

It wasn't hard to find clips on Mr. Abrams, who seemed to be a darling of the New York press corps. When it came to profiling members

New York City high society, his name was all over the place. After three hours, I had managed to piece together a much fuller picture of who Tobias Abrams was.

What struck me the most after forty years in the publishing industry, Tobias was planning to enter politics. The *Herald-Tribune* ran a lengthy piece on his bid for New York City mayor in the coming elections. He apparently ran for councilman four years prior, unsuccessfully.

So who was funding his campaign? I was far from an expert on politics, but I'd always been interested in how the system worked. Was Mr. Abrams at the mercy of special interests who, in return for their support, were applying pressure to tarnish my name? Who could that be?

The homeless guy who gave me directions came in and sat down at the opposite end of the table, concealing his brown bag. I waved.

"Howdy, kid," he said, showing me a toothless grin. "I see you found the place."

"Yeah," I said. "Thanks to you!"

"Hey, anything I can do to promote the literacy of our nation's youth." He seemed proud of himself for that statement and returned to his crumpled newspaper.

For the next hour, I looked everywhere for clues on who might have a special interest in Abrams' mayoral campaign. No names were jumping out at me. The city papers seemed very tight-lipped on the subject. I guess for a pretty good reason—if Abrams was being pressured by someone, he no doubt wanted to keep this information under wraps. And anyway, if he was as rich as he seemed to be, he probably didn't need any donation. He could fund the whole damn campaign himself.

The homeless guy coughed and walked toward my end of the table. He waved his newspaper in my face.

"Nothin' but killin' and stealin', killin' and stealin'. What a mess we've made of the world we live in, huh?" He spit on the floor. "I would give anything to be back in Indiana. At least there, the politicians are honest and the men aren't baby-killers." He was very close to my face and I could smell the liquor on his breath.

"Excuse me, sir," said the librarian, who had taken notice of our conversation. "I'm going to have to ask you to step outside."

He said, spitting again, "You can't even tell the truth in the library anymore." He shook his head and threw his paper down on the table in front of me. "Mark my words, son—the written word ain't nothin' but trouble." He held his brown paper bag tightly as he ambled out of the library under the librarian's watchful eye.

Maybe he's right, I thought to myself. The guy was clearly nuts, but maybe I was wasting time looking through pages and pages of empty words.

I started to put the magazines back on the shelves, careful to file them correctly as the librarian was now watching me suspiciously. I picked up the man's discarded newspaper and started to throw it away when something caught my eye.

There, in the middle of the page, was the following headline in bold:

YANKEES GM MARTIN FLETCHER ENDORSES ABRAMS FOR MAYOR.

This just got a whole lot more interesting. I began to read.

CHAPTER 17

The Last Supper

Howie McPherson sat on the edge of his chair, ill at ease in Fletch's office.

"I think you know why I'm here," Mac said.

"I guess I do," he replied.

Mac said, "I don't know how something like this happened, Fletch. This isn't the kind of publicity we need."

Fletch said, "Seems to me you boys fouled up your research. Didn't I ask you to get the dirt on David Roth?"

Mac reddened. "I guess we screwed up," he stammered, searching for an answer.

"I asked you both if this guy was clean. You said he was. Obviously, he wasn't." Fletch puffed leisurely on his cigar.

Mac noticed that Fletch wasn't exactly upset over the bad publicity. Quite the contrary, he seemed almost pleased.

"Casey mentioned something about gang activity," Fletch said, "but I can only assume neither of you dug down too deeply. It appears someone at *Look* magazine did. At least someone is doing their job."

"Sorry," Mac mumbled. Mac was accustomed to being able to smooth-talk his way out of almost any situation, he was a very powerful man. But when sitting face-to-face with Fletch, he found himself stumbling all over his words.

"What do you think this does to the Red Sox game?" Fletch finally asked.

Mac answered, "It puts a pretty nasty stain on Roth's record, that's for sure," he began quietly. "The Sox have Ted Williams. The guy's a war hero and is America's darling back in town just in time to play

America's favorite pastime." Fletch sucked on his cigar, a master at heightening the suspense. Fletch said, "Meanwhile, we've got a pitcher who's a warlord in the South Bronx and knocked off his girlfriend in a rumble gone awry."

Fletch shrugged. "You tell me, Mac. What do you think this does to the Sox game?"

Mac shifted uncomfortably in his seat. "I guess it doesn't do much for our image."

Fletch let out a growl. "That's for damn sure."

"Tell you what we should do," Mac began, hoping to land upon a solution as he was speaking. "Let's...let's publicly withdraw our support. Let's make it clear to the press that we had no idea about the questionable parts of Dave Roth's background. We never would have invited the kid to play for the Yankees—or even a Minor League team—if we'd known. Let's make it an issue of full disclosure—of Dave's failure to fully disclose his past."

Fletch stroked his chin. This gave him the air of deliberating the issue at hand, when of course this was exactly what he had in mind.

"What a shame it's come to this," Fletch said, with a big sigh. "But I don't see how we have any other choice. We can't sacrifice the whole organization's image for the sins of one player."

"Absolutely. That's exactly how I feel," Mac said, relieved to have stumbled across a plan that got himself off the hook.

"Good," Fletch said with finality. "Then it's settled. Drop Roth from the roster for next week's game. Pull up another pitcher from a Triple A club. Why we were even thinking of having a class D kid pitching this game is beyond me. Hell, get me anyone with a pulse and a fastball. But let me be clear, find someone who doesn't have a criminal record, for chrissakes."

"One more thing," Fletch added, savoring the look of shame on Mac's face. Putting the Yankees owner in his place was one of his favorite pastimes. "I also don't think Roth should play in the exhibition game with the Yankees tomorrow."

"Agreed. Of course not." Mac said.

"You'll deliver the news personally," Fletch said. "About both the exhibition and next week's game."

Mac swallowed hard. "I'm the owner, after all."

"I guess that's it then." Fletch threw his hands up in the air, the perfect picture of surrender. "What more can we do?"

"I guess that's all we can do." Mac stood up, eager to get out of Fletch's office.

"Good. Then it's settled." Fletch said.

He started to go, then paused for a moment.

"Also, Fletch…" Mac began. "I saw your piece in the *Trib* this morning. About you endorsing Abrams."

Fletch remarked, "Did you?" For a moment, Fletch worried that Mac was smarter than he thought.

Mac said, "I think that was very smart, actually, brilliant. It's the perfect angle to pitch—you supporting the President and Publisher of *Look*. Like you're very grateful to them for bringing this issue to light and helping us get rid of a bad seed, but at the same time, keep the New York Yankees' record spotless. It makes for a perfect story."

"Glad you think so," Fletch said, trying hard not to smile.

"Well, I should probably go," Mac said. "The Olean Yankees' management is handing out bonus checks to their players tonight. Final team dinner. I'm supposed to make an appearance. Guess I'll talk to Dave Roth while I'm there."

"Perfect," Fletch said. "Glad I can count on you, Mac. By the way… no bonus for Roth."

As Mac hurried out the door, the Yankees GM was grinning from ear to ear.

On the trolley back to the hotel, I didn't even notice St. Mary's Park or St. Rock's Cathedral flying by outside the window—I was too deep in thought. Every ounce of my mental concentration was being used to replay the *Trib* article over and over in my mind.

So Mr. Fletcher was a fan of Mr. Abrams. So much a fan that he was endorsing his mayoral campaign and I could only assume he had

THE LAST SUPPER

put an unspecified amount of money toward his campaign expenses. The picture in the *Trib* had showed the two men grinning and shaking hands in front of Yankee Stadium. It was from today's paper, so it was obviously current.

In the article, Abrams went on and on about his long-standing friendship with Fletcher and his lifelong appreciation of baseball. Fletch went on and on about Abrams being a fine leader in the New York literary world, and how he would surely continue his legacy of leadership as mayor. They were piling such huge compliments on each other that I smelled a rat under the garbage. My street instincts were kicking in big-time. The biggest flatterers were always the ones who would be the first to stick a knife in your back.

I thought it seemed strange that Fletch would support a cover story that put one of his players down. Unless there was an underlying motive.

It was a troubling thought. I was still kicking it around when I got back to the hotel, just in time to head up to my room and throw on a clean shirt and jacket for dinner with the team.

Candle was adjusting his tie in the mirror when I came in.

"Hey Dave," he said, his face brightening when I walked in the room. "We missed you today out on the field. It was a great workout, but it didn't feel right without you there."

"Yeah," I said. "I missed you guys, too."

"Where'd you go? I was worried about you." Candle said.

"You saw the article, right?"

Candle nodded solemnly. "We all saw it. It's horrible."

Dave said, "Tell me about it. Your family see it, too?"

The look on Candle's face answered my question. "But I told them it wasn't true and that you did not kill your girlfriend. They know what really happened."

I sank down on the edge of the hotel bed and asked, "Does it matter what really happened? Every magazine and newspaper in New York City is publishing their own version of the story. And people believe what they want to believe."

"It's a horrible thing that's happened," Candle said. "But I know it's going to be alright. There is a saying in the Bible: *y conoceréis la verdad, y la verdad os hará libres.* Then they will know the truth, and the truth will set you free."

I told Candle about my day at the library and the research I did.. Then I told him about the *Trib* article. As I told him about the strange liaison between Fletch and Abrams, his face darkened.

"This is very strange, Dave," he said. "In my country, this would be a very bad omen if the GM of a baseball team got very close to a politician. Of course, in my country, it's hard to find a politician who isn't corrupt."

"It's not so different here," I said. "It's something about money and power. When you got a lot of both of it, things tend to go wrong."

Candle thought for a moment. "It doesn't make sense that Fletch would want to damage your reputation. Unless…" He didn't finish his sentence.

"Unless what?" I asked.

Candle knitted his brows. "I've heard some things about Fletch that are not so good."

"What do you mean?"

Candle answered, "Everybody says that Fletch is a bigot."

"Really?" I said.

Candle said, "Think about it, amigo. Jackie Robinson broke the color barrier in 1947. It was all over newspapers, even in South America. There were so many good black players in the Negro League—Willie Mays, Hank Aaron, Roy Campanella. And they were all available. But not a single one of them ended up playing for the New York Yankees."

I had to admit that Candle was right. I never thought about it before, but the Yankees were a very white team. The handful of Italian-Americans—Vic Raschi, Yogi Berra, Phil Rizzuto, Bill Renna, Frank Verdi—were about as diverse as they got.

"If you put two and two together," Candle went on, "you start to wonder why Fletch didn't grab any of that great talent. It's been six years since Robinson signed with the Dodgers, and the Yankees still have no Negro players."

"So maybe Fletch is intentionally ignoring these players because of

THE LAST SUPPER

the color of their skin," I said.

"My point exactly." Candle responded.

"Gee, Candle" I said. "It makes me wonder if the powers that be in New York City have made a point to keep this out of the press. I've never heard this kind of speculation before, but it makes so much sense. Maybe New York City doesn't want to admit that the Yankees GM is a racist and a bigot."

Candle grinned, and I was glad to lighten the mood a little. Together we went downstairs.

A hush fell over the dining room the moment I entered. Skip and Shultzy looked up, and so did most of the other guys. Tom Rizzo was also there. He gave me a little nod. It was clear the other players weren't quite sure how to react to me. Was I still Dave, their friend and teammate, the nice guy they got to know in Olean? Or was I a former warlord in the South Bronx who had murdered his girlfriend?

Candle went to sit with his family, and I sat down next to C, who graciously made room for me at his table.

"Hey, man," he said, with an encouraging smile. "Don't worry. You've always got a place here."

"Thanks," I said, grateful to have at least two true friends. It was my last supper with my friends from Olean, and that damn article had robbed me of any enjoyment I might have gotten out of it. Instead of celebrating with the guys, I felt like an outsider—a kid off the streets who wasn't really welcome at the king's feast.

Shultzy and Rizzo made their way to the front of the room and Shultzy stepped up to the podium. I wished they would let us eat before the talk. All of my anger, frustration and anxiety had turned into one thing, hunger. I was starving.

"Gentlemen," Shultzy said, in a tone so formal it made me want to laugh, "you all know Tom Rizzo, the Yankees publicity director, who's here to help us celebrate this momentous occasion. We're so proud of all of you. But let's eat first, then talk."

"Hip, hip, hooray!" the guys shouted. I guessed everyone else was just as hungry as I was.

When everyone was through with their meal, Shultzy got up and started to talk again. "The Team of Destiny made Minor League baseball history this year. Your focus and behavior—in Olean and around the PONY League—was exemplified by your performance on and off the field. You've set an incredible example and standard for the entire Minor League system. In that spirit, the New York Yankees would like to thank each of you with a five hundred dollar bonus. As I call out your name, please come up to the podium and get your check from Tom Rizzo."

Five hundred bucks was huge. I planned on giving Mom and Dad the check to help them pay off their debt, the debt that I caused.

One by one, Shultzy called my teammates up to the podium, where he shook their hands. Then they received their checks from Rizzo and posed for a picture as the photographer crouched on the floor.

With every name he called, Shultzy gave each player a personal compliment and informed him where he'd be playing next season.

"Cecil Flood, you're a fine person and player. Next season, you'll be assigned to the Norfolk Tar Heels, in the class-B Piedmont League."

"Rocky Tunina, you are a delight and a very important part of the Olean Yankees. Next season, you'll be assigned to the Binghamton Twins in the class-A Eastern League."

"Roman Vilchez, you are a Major Leaguer in the making if ever I saw one. You'll be assigned to the Richmond Yankees in the class-AAA International League. You'll also be invited to spring training with the New York Yankees in St. Petersburg, Florida. Congratulations."

Candle was beaming. "I'm very happy," he said as he pumped Shultz's hand, and it sure showed. "Thank you, sir."

All of my teammates were getting the recognition they deserved, and I couldn't have been more proud of them. It was exciting news all around. Everyone was smiling.

Finally, my name was called. "I purposely saved Dave for last," Shultzy said as I walked up to the podium. A stillness had fallen over the room, and the distance between me and Shultzy seemed endless. "Dave's had to fight some pretty tough odds to get where he is today. But I think anyone who knows Dave would say that he's a champion ballplayer and an all-around great guy."

I appreciated Shultzy's vote of confidence, though I could tell the room was divided. It wasn't just the *Look* cover that had made them doubt me—it was the glut of headlines that had flooded the streets of New York when the afternoon and evening papers came out. With all the bad press I was getting, I knew that plenty of my teammates were no longer sure if I was such a great guy.

Mr. Rizzo handed me the check and shook my hand. Then he did something different than what he did with my teammates. He took the microphone.

"Dave, we're very proud that you'll be the first Jewish ballplayer to play in the big leagues with the New York Yankees. Welcome to this great organization, whose doors are wide open to all. You'll be signing your Major League contracts for 1953 and '54 tomorrow afternoon. Congratulations from the very top of the New York Ya—"

"Excuse me!"

We all whirled around to see who was speaking. There, standing in the doorway and panting heavily, was Howie McPherson, the owner of the New York Yankees.

"Sorry I'm late," he said, making his way to the podium. "I'm afraid I need to speak to the two of you. There's been a change of plans."

Mac, Rizzo, and Shultz stepped away from the podium and began a spirited discussion in the corner of the room. The rest of the room tried to act like we weren't watching, but it was impossible not to. None of us could hear what they were saying, but we didn't need to—we could tell that it wasn't a good discussion. Shultzy was becoming increasingly agitated the more animated Mac got. Rizzo stood with his arms folded, looking displeased.

Meanwhile, I stood by the podium, holding my check and wondering if I should go sit down. I wasn't sure whether or not their discussion had anything to do with me, but I had a bad feeling that it did.

After a few minutes, they motioned me over.

"Dave, I'm sorry we have to do this," Rizzo said, "but Mr. McPherson needs to have a word with you."

Mac coughed. "David Roth," he said, "the Yankees management must regretfully inform you that, due to misrepresenting yourself and your prior activities, we are revoking your bonus check and your Major League contract. You will also not play in the exhibition game tomorrow, either."

Shultzy was shaking his head furiously. "This isn't fair. This really isn't fair, damnit! At least give the kid a chance to clear his name."

Rizzo was silent. Mac shifted his weight, and I almost felt bad for him. He looked like he genuinely regretted being the one chosen to deliver the news.

I felt a burning rage begin to rise inside me, but I tempered it down. This wasn't the time or the place for it. If I wanted to clear my name, it wouldn't be by blowing up in front of the team owner.

"I understand, sir," I said. "I completely understand. You're doing what you have to do. I would do the same thing if I were in your shoes, sir." I paused. "I just have one question." The three men looked expectantly at me. "Is this what Martin Fletcher wanted?"

"Absolutely," McPherson said, looking relieved. "I just came from his office, as a matter of fact. He and I agree that this is what's best for the organization."

I nodded. "Then I'll leave with no questions asked. I want to do what's best for everyone."

I laid the check down on the table. As I did, I heard a murmur go through the crowd. Out of the corner of my eye, I caught Candle's glance. He looked more furious than Shultzy and Rizzo put together.

"I'm going to go now," I said quietly. "Thank you for your hospitality and dinner. It's been a great run, and I'll always remember my summer with the Olean Yankees. Thank you all."

Before anyone could protest, I walked out of the dining room, out of the hotel, and into the steamy New York night. I had work to do!

CHAPTER 18

The Big League Bigot

I spent the night at my folks apartment. I hardly slept a wink, tossing and turning for hours. I couldn't wait to get to the library the next morning and see if I could prove the theory that was rapidly forming in my mind. By eight o'clock the next morning, I was in the New York Public Library on 42nd Street in Manhattan. I read every piece of news I could on the Yankees after Martin Fletcher had been promoted to GM. I searched the baseball stats and wrote down the name of every single player under his watch. After four hours of focused research, I had my answer.

Since 1947—the year Fletcher became GM—the Yankees hadn't had a single Jewish player on the big league club. In the Minors, sure, but no Jew had reached the Major League level. The organization itself wasn't anti-Semitic. Not by a long shot. Nobody on our team ever gave me a hard time because I was a Jew. At the same time, whenever the bench jockeys on opposing teams gave me a hard time, my teammates always stood up for me. Sometimes with catcalling back at the loudmouths and sometimes with their fists after the game. So my conclusion was the Yankee organization did not have an anti-Semitic attitude.

But one man did. Fletcher.

Even more remarkable: the last Jewish ballplayer, Herb Karpel, had pitched for the Yankees in 1946. He played two games in the big leagues and was unceremoniously let go a few months later...when Fletcher moved up to the glass office.

Everything was lining up perfectly, like a nine-pitch, one-two-three inning. The *Look* article, having my contracts revoked, Fletcher's buddy-buddy relationship with Abrams for the benefit of the press—it all boiled down to one simple truth, Fletcher was a bigot. And it wasn't just black players he didn't want. It was Jews too.

My head was spinning as I walked home from the library. It was a lot to process. The whole thing was so simple, yet so unthinkable that I didn't want to believe it. But in my heart of hearts, I knew it all made sense.

I decided to go to Mom and Dad's again. When I finally got there, I peeked around the corner and saw that the reporters had camped out on our stoop. Those jerks, I thought to myself. They would do anything for a story. Instinctively I scanned the crowd for Sandy, but I didn't see any blondes in the crowd.

To avoid the press, I turned and went to Tony's. I needed to vent, and Tony was the perfect person for me to talk to. Candle was at Yankee Stadium with the rest of the guys, probably warming up for the exhibition game. I felt a pang of sadness thinking about how I was supposed to be out on that field, too. I was going to get back to Yankee Stadium by keeping a positive attitude. I was a long way from giving up. No one was taking this opportunity away from me—not even Martin Fletcher.

As I approached Tony's, I noticed a lone figure sitting on a suitcase near the entrance. For a moment, my heart stopped. Oh, no! Someone must have tipped the news guys off to my favorite hangout. I just wanted them to leave me alone!

As I got closer, I realized that it wasn't a reporter. At least, it didn't look like one. It appeared to be a girl in a bright red hat, sitting on top of a gray suitcase.

"Dave!" she called to me as I got closer. When I saw her green eyes flash, I recognized her instantly.

"Debbie!" I said, surprising myself with how glad I was to see her. She opened her arms wide and threw them around me, and I held her close for a long, long time, and I could feel her smiling, even though I couldn't see her face. She smelled just like she had that night at the Tavern—like vanilla and roses. I buried my face in her hair. I knew I had a real friend in her.

"It's so good to see you," I said. "I didn't realize how much I've missed you."

"And it's only been a few days!" she teased. "Actually, I know just what you mean. I've missed you too!"

"How did you get to New York City?" I asked.

"Took the train," she said proudly. "As soon as I read yesterday's news, I bought a train ticket immediately. I figured you could use some backup."

"Debbie," I said, "you're wonderful. I'm so sorry you had to find out about my past like that. I should have told you everything when we were together. The only reason I didn't was that it was painful for me to remember and talk about. Please understand that everything the reporters have been writing isn't true. They don't have the whole story."

She put her arms around my neck and gave me a long, passionate kiss.

"David Roth," she said. "Don't think for a minute that I am naive enough to believe everything I read. You are a good man, and I knew that from the first moment I laid eyes on you three months ago. Nothing any stupid reporter could put in print will ever change that. Got it?"

If I had to pinpoint the moment I fell in love with Deborah Simpson, that probably would have been it.

"Got it," I said, grateful to have her support. "But wait—how did you know I would be here?"

She grinned. "I may be a small-town girl, but I've got some big-city smarts. The reporters were buzzing around your parents' apartment something awful, so I did a little detective work of my own and found out where you typically hung out in the Bronx. I've been here for about an hour, hoping that sooner or later you would show up."

Debbie was full of surprises. "Wow," I said admiringly. "You're something else."

"Now why don't you buy me a Coke," she said, nodding toward Tony's, "and we can talk all about it?"

I grinned. "Sounds like the best idea I've heard in days." I pointed to her grey suitcase. "Is this coming with us?"

"We should probably take it in inside." She said. "My best friend graduated from Olean High last year and moved here to go to Sarah Lawrence College. I figured I would stay with her for a few days. But I wanted to find you first."

"I'm glad you did." I picked up the suitcase and we walked inside. I introduced Debbie to Tony. He liked her immediately and said, "The Cokes are on me."

Over slices of Tony's homemade apizza and two bottles of ice cold Coke, I filled Debbie in. I told her what had really happened that night at St. Mary's, including the name of Irena's actual killer. I caught her up on everything that had happened since we left Olean and everything I learned. When I finished talking, she shook her head.

"I hate to say it, but I think you're right. Sounds like Mr. Fletcher has something against you because you're Jewish." She brought her hand down hard on the bar countertop.

"What a fool he is. It makes me sick when people are victims of unfair prejudices. Especially someone as wonderful as you. You don't deserve this." She said.

"I guess I'm only the latest in a long line of people Fletcher has screwed. Pardon my language," I said.

Debbie put her hand over mine. "Don't worry—my father was in the navy. I've heard worse."

"Okay. Well, I was always taught not to swear when a lady's present." I let out a low whistle. "And you're quite a lady."

Debbie blushed. I didn't think it was possible that she could look any prettier, but when I saw the color rush to her cheeks, I realized I was wrong.

"Anyway, first Fletcher was against the Negro players, and he got his way by never signing any of them to the Yankees. For whatever reason, he agreed to give me my shot...only to sabotage me a few days later."

Debbie shook her head at the injustice of it all. She said, "It would have been better if he never called you up. To give you this shot and then take it away, that's very cruel."

"No kidding. He's playing dirty, that's for sure." I said.

Debbie responded, "If only there were some way to get him to confess to his dirty deeds."

I gave Debbie a look. "How on earth could we do that?" I asked.

She shrugged. "Beats me! But it sure would be great." She said.

I took another sip of my Coke and told her, "I'm afraid it's a pipe dream, Debbie. I couldn't even get up to Mr. Fletcher's office, let alone get the guy to confess to being a bigot. The way I see it, to get out of this mess, is to prove that I'm innocent. If I can show beyond a shadow of a doubt that I didn't kill Irena, then they'll have to retract every piece of news that calls me a murderer. Surely then the Yankees will issue an apology and welcome me back on the team…I think."

Debbie said, "Maybe. Or maybe not. If Fletcher is determined to keep you from playing, I bet he'll find some other way. Or he'll say fine, you didn't kill anyone…but you were a member of a gang and that's reason enough to keep you from playing. Or the fact that you have a criminal record. Any number of things. That's why I think we should go straight to the top."

"Well as soon as you think of a way, you let me know," I said.

She grinned. "Be careful giving me a challenge, Dave Roth. I just might rise to the occasion and surprise you!"

"I don't doubt it." I put my arm around her. "For now, let's focus on the first step, clearing my name."

Debbie offered. "Why don't you just give Big Joe up, Dave? Sounds like everybody knows he did it anyway. So what's it matter if you confirm what people already know?"

I responded, "It's gang code. I can't really explain it, but it has to do with honor. When you're in a gang with someone, you're like brothers. Even if you leave the gang—and even if they do something to betray you—you don't rat out a brother."

Debbie said, "Okay. I don't really understand but I've never been part of a gang."

Just then, we heard someone come in the door behind us. I turned around to see none other than Connor O'Neill, who was wearing his blue Wildcat bandana under his baseball hat.

"Hello, David," he said when he saw me. He emphasized David, like he was making a point not to call me Davey or do anything that might be mistaken for a sign of friendship. "Who's the broad?"

"This is Debbie," I said. She extended her hand for Connor to shake. He ignored it. Oh man, I thought. He's really not getting off on the right foot with me.

Connor said, "Looks like the papers blew up with bad news blues," he said. "Guess that's what happens when you try to cover up your mistakes, they come back to bite you in the butt."

I could feel my heartbeat starting to speed up like it always did when I got angry. I said, "My mistakes? I think you need to watch what you say, Connor. I would be careful about pointing fingers and assigning blame."

Connor responded, "Be careful about who you're talking to. You're not warlord of the Wildcats anymore."

"And I don't want to be. That's the whole point." I answered.

I suddenly remembered what Tony and I had talked about the day before—that deep down, Connor respected my position as a former warlord and was threatened by it. I got up from my chair. Debbie put her hand on my arm and whispered, "Be careful, Dave." I gave her a nod to let her know everything would be okay.

"Connor, you're a good kid," I said. "And you're too bright to be throwing your life away. You should be in school finishing your education, not picking fights on the street."

"Don't talk down to me," Connor said. "You want to fight me? Then fight me. But don't lecture me about school."

"I don't want to fight you. I don't want to fight anyone. That's why I left gang life. It's not fun and games—it's flesh and blood. It's people getting hurt and people dying. Have you ever been in a rumble, Connor?"

He answered, "No. But I've kicked butt in every fight I've ever been in."

"It's not the same thing as going head-to-head with some guy by the flagpole after school. A rumble is a whole other ball game. Have you ever used a knife? Have you ever gotten stabbed by one?"

I could tell from his silence that he hadn't. "Take a look at this." I peeled my shirt back from my shoulder and showed him the ugly gash in my flesh where Alejandro had plunged his knife. Even though it had healed relatively well, the scar still looked intense. It was more than two inches long, jagged and white. I heard Connor take a deep breath.

"Does that look like it was fun?" I asked, not expecting Connor to answer the question.

"No," he said, his voice a lot lower.

"Is there a girl you like?" I asked him.

His face softened, and for a moment, the tough-guy facade all but faded away. "There's a girl I kind of like at school, yeah." He swallowed his emotion and hardened again. "But what does it matter?" He looked at Debbie and said, "We all got a broad. They're easy to come by."

"Listen to me," I said. "A good woman is damn hard to find. They only come along every so often. And when you got one, you gotta hang on for dear life." I answered.

I cast a smile over my shoulder at Debbie, who responded in kind. I turned back to face Connor. "Do you know what it's like to watch someone you love be killed?"

His face whitened. "No. I guess I don't."

"Well it's the worst kind of pain you'll ever experience. A lot worse than this," I said, pointing to the scar on my shoulder. "It's like getting your heart ripped out of your chest, over and over and over again. The pain never completely goes away—it just changes."

I could tell that Connor was trying to play it tough, but what I was saying was getting to him. And no wonder—he couldn't be older than seventeen. He was trying to act all macho and grown up, but underneath he was just a scared kid who was in over his head. I knew exactly how he felt, because I was that same kid once.

"I've seen things you can't even imagine, man," he said to me. "You don't know the kind of stuff that goes on at my house. You have no idea. I've seen violence, okay? I'm not some skirt. I've seen some awful stuff."

Considering everything I'd heard about Mr. O'Neill, Connor and Big Joe's father, I figured he was probably right.

"Okay," I said, acknowledging what he had said. "I believe you. But then why would you want to cause more violence? Why would you want to keep doing the same things when you've seen how devastating it can be?"

For a second I thought I'd really gotten through to him. He looked like he wanted to give me a big hug and cry a little. But then his walls went right back up and he set his lips in a hard line.

"Screw you and your pep talks, Dave," he said. "You're trying to fill my head with lies so that I'll chicken out and you can take control of the Wildcats. That's why you came back to the Bronx. My brother always said you were two-faced. Wait till I tell him all the crap you've been feeding me."

My mouth fell open, but I quickly shut it again. If Connor was going to talk to Big Joe about this conversation…it meant he knew where Big Joe was.

"You're going to tell Big Joe about this?" I asked, trying to play it cool.

"Damn right I am," Connor said, still blowing off steam. "He always said you Jews weren't to be trusted. We'll see what he has to say about you trying to stage a takeover—" He stopped himself mid-sentence. I had a feeling he realized he already said too much.

"I'm outta here," he said. He pointed a menacing finger in my direction. "I'll be seeing you."

The minute he left, Debbie rushed over to me.

"Did you hear what he said, Dave?"

"I sure did."

"Looks like we just get one step closer to proving your innocence," she said excitedly. "Turns out Big Joe isn't MIA after all."

"Exactly." I said. "Sounds like he's either lying low in town—or his brother at least knows where he is."

"You up for a little adventure?" Debbie asked grabbing my hand. "C'mon. Let's follow him."

A week ago she was Debbie the waitress in the Olean Diner. Now, here in the South Bronx, she was Debbie the Detective. And it was exciting.

We spotted Connor high-tailing it down the street.

"Shhhh," she said, giving me a flirtatious wink.

"Maybe this whole 'clearing my name' thing won't be so bad after all." I said.

CHAPTER 19
Debbie The Detective

Debbie and I walked cautiously on East 149th Street, making sure we kept out of Connor's sight. Every now and then, when Connor paused, we hid behind anything we could find. Once we found ourselves in a women's underwear store, that was tacky.

"I'd like to see you in some of these." Dave said.

"You're distracting me." Debbie whispered.

"Why's that?" Dave asked.

"Because I'm getting excited," Debbie confessed.

She giggled and dragged me toward the door until we were out of the shop and back on Connor's tail.

For a warlord, Connor's street smarts could have used some sharpening up. He was being followed by two giggling teenagers and he was totally clueless. I kept expecting him to turn around and tell us to take a walk, but he never did. He just kept walking straight ahead, oblivious to the world around him.

After several blocks, Connor took a sharp right turn down an alley. Debbie and I were close on his heels.

"Where do you think he's going?" she asked.

"We're about to find out." I answered.

We shadowed Connor as he walked down the alley, wondering if he was going to dart into a back door or climb up a fire escape. My adrenaline was pumping, and I was just waiting for Connor to make a definitive move. He popped out the other end of the alley and abruptly turned left.

We rushed after him, he was nowhere in sight.

"Damn!" I said. "We lost him."

"No, we didn't," Debbie said. She pointed to the store immediately to our left.

"Look inside."

And there he was, sitting at the counter of an ice cream parlour, smiling at the pretty girl scooping up chocolate ice cream into a cone.

I let out a low whistle. "Well I'll be damned. It seems that even warlords have a sweet tooth."

Debbie laughed. "Is it funny that we just tailed a guy on his way to get ice cream?"

"I feel like a scoop of butter pecan myself." I pretended to be about to go inside.

"Dave!" Debbie threw herself in front of me. "We can't go in or he'll know we're following him!"

"Relax! I'm just playing. I won't blow our cover." I ducked out of view and leaned against the brick wall beside the store. I pulled her against me. "I kind of like this game," I said. "Watching you play detective is better than reading Marvel Comics."

Debbie started to say something, but then she stopped.

"What were you going to say? I hope I didn't offend you. It's just that I'm so happy to have your friendship." I told her.

I saw that Debbie seemed distracted. She wasn't looking at me, she was looking inside the ice cream parlor.

"Dave," she whispered. "Something's going on in there."

"What do you mean?" I angled my body so I could see into the shop windows.

Debbie was right. Inside the shop, Connor was still talking to the girl behind the counter, but they weren't smiling anymore. Their heads were very close together and they looked like they were in the middle of an intense conversation. Then the girl started waving her arms over her head. She was pretty angry about something. As her voice rose, Debbie and I could pick up pieces of what she was saying.

"Doesn't WANT to talk to you...not SAFE...told him he should... doesn't trust you...what do YOU know?"

By this point, both Debbie and I had our ears pressed up against the glass. Lucky for us, we were partially hidden by a large refrigerator inside the shop. The good news was that they couldn't really see us, the bad news was our view was restricted as well. We struggled to piece together the girl's side of the conversation. Then Connor started to yell.

"I TOLD you I need to...won't be a problem...trying to mess with... have to talk to...I'm his BROTHER, Rosanna!"

When I heard the word "brother," I froze. Debbie looked at me, her eyes wide.

"Oh my God," she whispered. "Dave...I think he's in there."

"What?" I was still trying to make sense of the snippets we were hearing.

"I think Big Joe is really in there." Debbie said.

"In the ice cream parlor? Why would he be in there?" I asked.

I could almost see Debbie's brain working in overdrive as she pulled all the pieces together and said, "It must be his girlfriend. Or a good friend or something. Someone he knew he could trust. So he's been hiding out in her shop. Maybe there's a room upstairs and she brings him food so that he never has to go out. Or maybe he did leave town, but then he got tired of living in exile so he decided to come back and lay low for a while. Now this girl is stowing him away, and the only other person who knows he's here is, is Connor."

I looked at her in admiration and said, "You're good. Where did you learn all this detective stuff?"

She shrugged. "I read a lot of Nancy Drew books as a kid. Though, to be honest...I always enjoyed the Hardy Boys more."

"So now what?" I said, eager to take action. "I think I should go in there and confront them."

She shook her head. "Not yet. You're courageous, Dave...it's one of the things I like about you. But let's gather as much information as we can before we make our move."

We didn't have to wait long. The next thing we knew, Connor was rushing toward the exit. We barely had time to jump into Bob's Electrical Supply Shop before he ran by.

"Phew," Debbie said, hiding behind a tall floor lamp. "That was close."

"You're tellin' me."

We were both breathing heavily, excited by our game of cat and mouse—the one we were playing with Connor O'Neill and the one we were playing with each other.

Suddenly I said, "Debbie, can I have a kiss?"

She thought for a moment. "Yes. But first, answer one question."

"Anything."

"If you had five minutes alone with Big Joe O'Neill, do you think you could get him to confess?"

That wasn't the question I was expecting.

I said to Debbie, "Big Joe and I had grown up together in the Bronx. He was always a trouble-maker and there is long-standing tension between us.

As we grew up, Big Joe was always trying to get me in trouble. He resented me for doing well in school, and by the time we both got involved with the Wildcats, he resented me for being a good athlete and well-liked by the rest of the guys. I knew he hated my leadership role, but the truth was that even the toughest gang members were scared of Big Joe. He was just too mean and unpredictable. He was like a bottle of Coke someone had shaken up—no one knew exactly when he was going to explode."

But now, thanks to Connor, I had a better picture of Big Joe's life than ever before. I knew his kid brother was warlord of the Wildcats, the position he wanted more than anything. If Debbie's instincts were correct, then he was hiding out in an ice cream parlor on East 148th Street. Judging by the fact the ice cream parlor girl didn't seem keen on the idea of Connor seeing his brother Big Joe, I was guessing that the relationship between them wasn't too hot.

Debbie said, "That was a lot of quality information. Could I do something with that? You bet."

"Yeah," I said. "Actually, I do. I think I know exactly what buttons to push to make Big Joe O'Neill talk."

Debbie beamed. "That's all I need to know." She pushed the lamp aside and marched straight out the front door.

"Hey, wait up!" I said, running after her as she walked briskly down the street.

"Miss me already?" Debbie called over her shoulder as I jogged to catch up to her.

I said, "You haven't seen anything yet. Just you wait and see. Debbie, you are something else! I'm not sure I've ever met a girl like you. You're funny, smart, brave...and beautiful, all wrapped up in one girl, Wow!"

"Thanks," she said, with a modest shrug. "You're not so bad yourself."

"So where are we off to now?" I asked.

"Actually, this is where we part ways."

"What?" I tried not to let my disappointment show, but it was obvious. It had been a miserable couple of days and I was finally getting my balance back. And now Debbie was leaving.

"Oh," I said. "So you're going back to Olean?"

"No, silly! We'll see each other later. I just mean, part ways for the time being. I've got a couple of errands I need to run."

"You do?" She had piqued my curiosity. "Like what?"

"You'll see," she said, obviously enjoying keeping me on the hook. "I'm sure you've got things to do, right?"

"Well, considering I was supposed to be playing an exhibition game against the Yankees right now…" I said.

"I'm sorry, Dave. I know how sad you must be feeling. You really love the game, don't you?" Debbie said.

"More than I can say." I answered.

"We'll get you back out there," she said with resolve. "I'm determined. And when I'm determined, no one better get in my way!"

I put my hands up in mock surrender. "I certainly won't!"

"Good." She grinned. "Where there's a will, there's a way. And I've got a mighty will. Even better—I've got an idea. But first I've got to do a little reconnaisance work. I've got to get you the right bat so you can hit a home run. You know what I mean?"

I didn't, but I loved the fact that Debbie was using baseball illustrations to make her point. She was so damn cute.

"So," she said, "I'm off. I'm going to go pick up my suitcase at Tony's and then take a cab to my friend's house. Then the real fun begins."

"Do you need an escort?" I said, hoping I might be able to steal more time with her. "The Bronx can be kind of dangerous, you know."

"I'm a big girl," she teased. "I think I can survive the big bad Bronx."

"I don't doubt it." I answered. "You know, your suitcase reminded me...I actually have an errand to run myself. I left the hotel in such a hurry last night, I didn't even get my stuff. Assuming they haven't thrown my duffle out on the front curb, it's probably still up in my room. Now's the perfect time for me to go get it since the rest of the team is out of the hotel.

I won't have to see anybody, which is good."

"That's probably best," she agreed.

"Perfect." I said. "Where should we meet up afterwards?"

"I may need until tomorrow, so let's set up a place to meet for a late lunch. Tony's again?" Debbie asked.

"Great. Unless someone tips off the reporters, that seems like a safe spot for a rendezvous. Let's meet there at two." I said.

"Good." Debbie said. "I'll miss you."

"And I'll miss you too."

There was something about kissing in the middle of East 148th Street, with the cars flying by all around us and the knowledge that together we were on a mission...it was passionate, exciting and almost unreal.

"I should go," she whispered. "I'll be thinking about you."

"I'm already thinking about you," I said, as Debbie walked out of sight.

CHAPTER 20
The Troubled Outcast

At the Concourse Plaza Hotel, I greeted the doorman.
"Hey, George," I said.

"Davey!" he said, seeming glad to see me. I made a point to talk to him every time we saw each other, so by this point, we were like old buddies. "We missed you today, man," he told me. "Where you been?"

"Long story. Let's just say I'm not out at Yankee Stadium with the rest of the guys, by choice."

"What the hell, they screwed you. You had it made in the shade. We've all been rooting for you. You're one of us playing in the big leagues!"

"Not today," I said. "Believe me, if it were up to me, I would be out there."

"I'm sorry to hear it." George shook his head. "That guy oughta get bent. You let me know if there's anything I can do, okay?"

"Okay. Thanks."

I felt a little better as I made my way up the stairs to my hotel room.

My key still worked—at least they hadn't changed the locks on me—and the door swung open. What I saw when I got inside our room just about made me cry.

Candle had taken the time to pick up all of my clothes and fold them neatly in a pile on my bed. He even matched up my socks. On top of the stack of clothes was a letter, amazingly written by Candle.

Dear Dave,

    I've gotten to know you over the last three months, and I can truly say that you are more than a teammate to me. You are a brother and a best friend. No matter who slanders you, I know who you really are and don't you forget it. You are Dave Roth, the best ballplayer I ever knew and the best man, too.

    If I don't see you again, please know that you always have a place to stay with me and my family in Venezuela. We miss you, Dave. Playing the Yankees today won't be the same without you.

Your friend,
Roman (Candle) Vilchez

I thought to myself how honored I felt to have met someone like Candle, who I know will be my friend for life.

I slung my duffle bag over my shoulder and headed downstairs, nodding to George on my way out. As I stood outside under the hotel canopy, I heard cheers coming from Yankee Stadium. The sound of 50,000 fans in the stands was unmistakable. I felt a knot the size of a catcher's mitt in my stomach.

"We can't tell you how much we appreciate this, John. Particularly on such short notice."

I heard a voice I recognized over my right shoulder, so I turned to see Mr. McPherson escorting someone into the hotel.

"Anything I can do to help the Yankees," the someone said. "Especially against those Red Sox." It didn't take me long to put a name to the voice and face. It was John Hare, the madman pitcher for the Jamestown Tigers.

The Yankees had obviously traded for him...to take my place!

Furious, I ducked behind a big white Cadillac so they wouldn't see me.

"You're really helping us out of a tight spot," Mr. McPherson said, as he ushered him to the lobby. George held the door open and neither Mr. McPherson or Hare acknowledged him. "After everything that's happened with Roth, we just couldn't afford any more bad publicity." McPherson said.

I couldn't believe it. They brought John Hare to the Yankees as my replacement? The guy who managed to make America's pastime violent and tried to kill me in Olean? It made my blood boil.

Then again, I thought, if they're looking for a bigot, look no further. John Hare's practically a young Martin Fletcher in the making.

George noticed me hiding behind the Cadillac. "Davey, is that you?"

"Yeah, Georgie. It's me."

"Who's that guy the Yankees owner just brought in?"

"He's my replacement," I said.

"What the hell?" He said.

George shook his head. "This is some fine baloney, Davey. Hows about a drink at the hotel bar?"

"That sounds great," I said, glad to have someone to talk to. It was beginning to feel like things couldn't get any worse.

George and I bonded over beers at the hotel bar. I shared with him how disappointed I was about everything, and how much I wanted to be out on the baseball diamond doing my thing.

"You're a star, Davey," he said. "You're already a Bronx legend, just from your stats in Olean this summer. But you deserve to be out there on the field, playin' with the big guys."

"I guess you never stop paying for some mistakes," I said.

"Bull," George said. "We've all got stuff in our pasts. It's just that someone has decided to rub your nose in yours."

"He's rubbed all of New York City's nose in it!" I said, thinking of Fletcher.

"So whatcha gonna do about it, kid?"

"I'm not sure yet," I said. "But something."

After a few more beers, we were both pretty blitzed. George had taken a much longer break than he was supposed to, but no one seemed to mind. I guessed that he was a veteran at the Plaza—he'd earned himself a long leash.

When we heard a ruckus outside, I figured the exhibition game must be over. Sure enough, the busses were pulling up and my teammates were piling out. Judging by the dejected looks on their faces, the

Olean Yankees had been defeated.

"I should scram," I said. "Probably better if they don't see me."

"Nah, just hang here a while," George said. "They ain't gonna see you."

He was right—the guys were so wrapped up in their loss that they didn't notice anything as they trudged upstairs to their rooms. I felt sorry for them. It was their last big hurrah in the Bronx, and it had ended on a down note. Damnit, I thought. If I was playing, I think I could have helped a little.

Then I noticed one figure wearing a red hat who didn't quite blend in to the crowd. To my surprise, it was Debbie, pushing her way through the guys.

"Candle!" she called. "Hey, Candle!"

I spotted Candle waiting for the elevator. He turned around when he heard his name, looking very surprised to see Debbie.

They spoke in low tones for a moment, and Debbie glanced several times over her shoulder. Finally, Candle smiled. The elevator door opened, and both Candle and Debbie stepped inside as the elevator doors closed. I watched the number light above. Three. The third floor. They were going to our room.

"Did you see that?" I asked George, hoping my eyes were playing tricks on me.

"That? Oh sure. Happens all the time. These girls go crazy over a guy with a ball and a bat. Nowadays a player gets more play off the field than he does on it, if you know what I mean." He grinned. "Why? He a friend of yours?"

"He was."

I tried to think of a reasonable explanation for why Debbie would go up to Candle's room, but I couldn't think of any. I knew they'd known each other in Olean, but to my knowledge it had never gone beyond hello's and "goodbye's at the diner. Even worse, Debbie knew Candle and I were good friends.

"I need a scotch," I told the bartender, who poured the drink with no questions asked.

What next? I wondered. I was booted off the team I loved, my future in baseball eliminated before it even started. My friends in the South Bronx wouldn't talk to me because they thought I was a coward for leaving our gang. My teammates from Olean wouldn't talk to me because they thought I was a murderer. Alejandro wanted to kick my butt, or kill me. The girl I was falling in love with was sneaking around behind my back with the guy I'd thought was my best friend. The GM of the Yankees had it out for me because I was Jewish, and to replace me they'd gone out and found my biggest rival in the Minor Leagues.

I had a sudden desire to go grab one of my old bats and crush something with it. The thought made me shudder. For the last year, I used a bat only to play baseball, never to fight. And now, when the chips were down, my old instincts were coming back to the surface. I was angry and hurt. It made me want to fight someone.

But you don't speak that language anymore, Davey, I reminded myself. That's the way you communicate if you're in a gang. But you're not in a gang anymore.

I nursed my scotch, wondering why all the people I cared about the most had betrayed me.

A few minutes later, the elevator doors slid back open and Debbie walked out. She looked flustered and excited, her cheeks rosy like they were earlier when I'd made her blush. Now that little display of modesty seemed so fake and ridiculous it almost made me cry. What a fool I am.

Debbie ran out the front door, and I wondered if Candle was congratulating himself. He got rid of me and got my girl, all in one fell swoop. What would Maria, his girlfriend, say? I felt like going to find her and telling her what a creep she had for a boyfriend. I couldn't believe that was Candle. After his phony sweet note and promises of forever friendship. What a joke. What a rotten joke! No wonder he'd folded up all my clothes—a guy does a lot of strange things when he's ridden with guilt. There really was nobody I could trust other than Mom and Dad.

I asked the bartender for another scotch. "Better make it a double," I said.

How quickly it all can change, I thought bitterly. A few days earlier,

I was on top of the world. Now everything was crumbling down all around me, and I had a front row seat.

"That bad, huh?" George asked, putting a hand on my shoulder.

"You have no idea."

CHAPTER 21

The Windup

I stayed up all night walking the streets in a daze. I finally went to Tony's to have a liquid breakfast. It didn't take long for Tony to come out from behind the bar and sit down beside me. Even though I was feeling no pain, I could tell he was concerned.

"I think you should go home, Davey," he said.

I didn't want to go—fought him all the way—but in the end, I gave in. He got someone to cover for him at the restaurant and walked me back to my folks' apartment himself. Most of the press had left by then, but a couple of stragglers had stayed behind, still hoping for a story. They tried to squeeze a few words out of me as I stumbled up the stoop, but Tony waved them away.

"I think you guys have done enough," he yelled, and something in his tone made them back off.

My parents were very happy to see me—they were worried sick wondering where I was. They stayed home from work to be with me in case I came home. They thanked Tony profusely as he went on his way. Mom led me by the hand and put me to bed on the sofa, where I slept as a kid. I couldn't bear to look at them because I was so embarrassed, I turned on my side and fell into a deep sleep.

Sometime early the next morning, I opened my eyes. For a split second, everything was a-okay. Then it all came back to me. Fletcher. Debbie. Candle. I rolled over and went back to sleep. I wasn't ready to face the world.

When I woke up again, it was 12:30. My head was pounding from the night before, so I went to the 92nd Street Y for a swim. It made me feel a little better. Even if everyone in the world betrayed me, at least

I could still swim. Then, as I was changing in the locker room, I did something I hadn't done in a couple of days. I got on my knees and prayed. I thanked God for everything he gave me and the wonderful summer I'd had in Olean. And then I asked him why he chose to take it all away.

I didn't get an answer, which was okay. I wasn't really expecting one.

Since I didn't have anywhere to be, I took a long walk back from the Y in Manhattan to the South Bronx, eventually wandering aimlessly down the streets of my neighborhood.

A few days before, my life had been full of potential and opportunity, now there was nothing to look forward to, nothing to work toward. Amazing, I thought, how quickly everything can change. I passed several groups of guys hanging on the street corners, wearing their gang colors with pride and talking tough. It occurred to me that maybe I would be stuck here, in the rough-and-tumble world of the South Bronx, for the rest of my life. Maybe this was my destiny all along.

I went back to my parents' apartment and got a ball, bat, and glove.

The wood felt good in my hands, cool and smooth. Man, I missed that feeling. There was no sound as beautiful as the smack of a ball against a bat, or the dull thud of a ball sinking into the catcher's mitt. I picked up my glove and touched it lovingly, wondering when I'd get to use it again.

Well, no one's stopping you, said a voice in my head. Give it a whirl, Davey.

That's how I ended up alone on a baseball field in Crotona Park, the field that Morris High School used. I started to pitch against an imaginary opponent with all my might. I imagined Eddie Lopat's strings as I did my windup, throwing one perfect pitch after another. Each time, I had to run to get the ball from the chain link fence that I was throwing to. It certainly wasn't very efficient, but it sure felt good to run. It felt good to be out on a field, doing what I loved, even if I was all alone doing it.

And then I heard the same voice in my head as before, only louder and clearer this time. You know who you are, Dave, it said. This is your game and your destiny. Don't ever give it up.

"Hello, Roth."

The sound of a real voice startled me. I turned around to see Alejandro standing just a few feet behind me. He was holding something in his right hand that glistened in the sun. My street instincts kicked in immediately. He was holding a switchblade.

"Surprised to see me?" Alejandro asked.

"Surprised to see you without your gang," I said. I thought about my options. I could try to run…but that's not who I am.

Alejandro said, "I figured we could do this…man to man." He flipped his blade around in his palm and caught it smoothly, showing off his skills with a knife. "I think you've seen this before."

I answered, "Yeah, in my shoulder. What the hell are you going to do, Alejandro? Stab me in the back again? Is that really how it's going to end?"

"For you, yes," he said with a grin. I watched him cautiously as he began to circle me. I was going to protect myself at any cost. I saw my bat leaning against the fence near home plate.

"I don't want to fight you," I said. "I really don't."

"Don't you want to go down like a man, Roth?"

"I'm more of a man than you'll ever be." I answered.

He reacted to my words by charging me with a battle cry. I sidestepped his attack and his momentum sent him hurling forward. I could have used the opportunity to grab my bat, but I suddenly felt very calm and confident..

"I don't want to fight you," I said again, this time a little louder.

"You keep saying that. Turn around and fight me like a man!" Alejandro said, his eyes blazing. "My cousin deserved better than a yellow kike."

Something snapped inside of me. I felt rage running through my body, the kind of rage that used to spike my adrenaline before a rumble. But instead of making me wild the way it used to, it was making me very steady.

"Your cousin deserved better than THIS," I said, my voice strangely low and powerful. "She deserved better than being caught between two stupid gangs of kids who hate each other for no reason. She also

The Windup

deserves better than a wild man who runs around using his knife to feel tough like a man."

Alejandro's eyes flashed with raw anger. He wanted to fight, and so did I. But I wasn't done yet. I had a few more choice things to say to him.

"And yeah," I told him, watching him carefully for a sudden move with the knife, "she deserved better than me—a boyfriend who loved her more than anything and didn't take care of her the way I should have, because I was too young and stupid to know how. She deserved to get out of this stupid neighborhood and this stupid city and away from these stupid gangs that killed her before she even had a decent shot at a real life." Alejandro was looking at me with his mouth open. He didn't know what to say.

"Irena deserved more than you gave her, and more than I gave her, and a hell of a lot more than all of us jerks gave her together." I shook my head. These thoughts had been banging around in my head for months, but it was the first time I'd ever said any of them aloud.

"I didn't shoot your cousin, Alejandro. For eighteen months now, I've sworn to myself that if I ever saw the guy who did, I'd kill him. But you know what? I wouldn't. I'm sick of killing. I'm sick of this crap, and it's time it stopped."

Alejandro was still holding his knife, but I could tell by his eyes that something changed. He was looking at me in a different way. It took me a moment to recognize it, and then I knew it instantly. He was looking at me with respect.

"Can we put an end to this?" I said, extending a hand. "I'm done with the Wildcats. I'm done with gangs. That part of my life is over. But for the sake of Irena...how about a truce between the Rockets and the Wildcats?"

Alejandro eyed my outstretched hand. Then he looked back up at me. He waited for what seemed like an eternity. Finally, he spoke.

"Roth," he said quietly, "You are more courageous than I knew. I surprised you here, all alone, and you have acted very bravely. I expected you to fight, and you did fight...but you fought with words. I respect that." He folded his knife and put it in his back pocket and said, "I won't fight you. Irena would have wanted it that way."

He looked at my hand again, then shook his head.

" My cousin's blood was shed by the Wildcats. You and I both know who did it."

I was stunned and said, "You know who had the gun?" All this time, I thought Alejandro had truly believed it was me who fired the weapon.

He said, "I've known all along. But you were the leader, it was your responsibility to make sure he didn't use it."

"I told him to leave it at home!" I exclaimed. "You don't know how many times I've played that night over in my head—what I could have done differently. What I should have done differently. But I can't rewind the clock. I can't change the past."

He said, "No. But a debt is a debt." He stepped in closer. "I know O'Neill is still in the neighborhood. I hear people talking. They say he's hiding somewhere. So the next time you see him, you give him a message from me. You tell him if he doesn't pay his debt, then his kid brother is going to pay for him."

There was something so menacing in Alejandro's eyes that I was speechless, unable to use reason and good sense against him.

"You tell him," he went on, "that if he doesn't give himself up for what he did, I'm coming for his brother. That kid doesn't know he's playing with fire—he's the greenest warlord I've ever seen. So you tell him, Roth…if he doesn't own up to spilling my cousin's blood, I'll spill his brother's. I'll put a knife in his heart."

"You don't have to do that, Alejandro," I said quietly. "There is another way."

He said, "Not for me, there isn't. You've got your baseball and your big shot friends. I ain't got none of that. This is my life, Roth. You think you're better than us? Fine. It's not your fight anymore. But I have a debt to settle with the O'Neills, and there's nothing you can say to change my mind."

I nodded, realizing that he was right—I wasn't going to be able to change his mind.

"Okay. I will deliver your message if I ever find him." I said.

Alejandro nodded. He turned to go, then paused. "Best of luck to you, Dave Roth," he said. "You and I are from different worlds. But I hope you make it back to the Yankees. You deserve it. You bring class and hope to all of us."

Before I could respond, Alejandro walked away.

I missed my lunch date with Debbie, but I didn't care. At the moment she was the least of my concerns. After my face-off with Alejandro, everything else had melted away and in its place was a die-hard resolve. I felt a new kind of energy flowing through my veins. I was determined, and I was unstoppable. If anyone was going to get me out of the mess I was in, it would be me.

Alejandro's final words echoed in my head. He was right, I had worked too hard to give up now. Playing with the Yankees was the most important thing in the world to me. No way was I going to let an anti-Semitic racist GM and some bad press take that away. I was done fighting with bats and knives. But I will never be done fighting for my dream.

I had a plan. First, I had to clear my name.

The ice cream parlor on East 148th Street was empty when I got there. When I walked in, a cowbell attached to the doorknob gave a little chime.

"Hi, can I help you?" A girl appeared from the back—the same girl Debbie and I had seen with Connor the day before. Her name tag read "Rosanna." I realized Rosanna was a few years older than us, maybe in her early twenties. She already had lines at the corner of her eyes, and she looked a little beat up. *Maybe she looks that way because she's hiding something, or someone*. I thought to myself.

"I hope you can," I replied. "I'm looking for someone."

"Oh?" she asked, smiling sweetly. "Who?"

"I think you know who."

For a moment, she froze. Then her smile was back, this time even sweeter than before. "Oh sure. You must mean my sister, Jeannie. Are you a friend from school?"

Suddenly it all made sense. I remembered Jeannie from Morris—a fiery redhead who was big-time trouble. Then I remembered that she and Big Joe had palled around a lot, stirring stuff up around the neighborhood. Their nickname at school was "Bonnie and Clyde." Jeannie must have talked her big sister into letting her boyfriend use the shop as a hideout.

"I know Jeannie," I said. "That's your sister?"

"Uh huh. She works here, too." She answered.

"It's your shop then?" I asked.

"I took it over when our father passed away." She answered.

"So you and Jeannie live here?" I asked.

"Yes," she said nervously. "We live above the shop. Anything else you want to know?"

"Actually, yeah," I said. "You and your sister live alone?"

"That's a pretty personal question," she said, tensing.

"It's only personal if you've got something to hide." I said.

Rosanna had stopped smiling. She laid both hands on the counter and looked at me calmly.

"Let's just cut to the chase here. Who are you, and what do you want?"

"My name is Dave Roth, and I'm not here to cause any trouble," I said. "I just want to speak to Big Joe."

Her eyes got very wide.

"I don't know what you're talking about," she said. "If Big Joe is a friend of Jeannie's then you need to take it up with my sister." She started to walk into the back of the shop but I grabbed her gently by the arm. She didn't try to get away, just stood very, very still.

"Rosanna," I said, "this can't be easy for you, either. You're harboring a criminal. Do you really want the police to shut down your shop? Do you want to go to jail?"

She shook her head and mouthed "No" so quietly that I could barely hear her from a foot away.

"Then it's time to stop playing."

I let go of her arm. She gave me a long, hard look, and I couldn't tell if she was going to agree with me or run.

"Wait here," she said.

Rosanna disappeared into the back of the shop. A minute later, she came back. "Come with me," she said, and took me to the back room. I stood blinking, waiting for my eyes to adjust to the dark.

"Hey, Davey."

I could just about make out a figure in the shadows. It was Big Joe O'Neill.

As my eyes slowly got into focus, I could hardly believe what I saw. This was a different Big Joe than the one I last saw in St. Mary's Park eighteen months ago. He was much skinnier, and he looked very pale. A true Irishman, Big Joe always had white skin and freckles, but his skin looked brown in the dark light.

I could now see in his eyes, that he was frightened. But as I stared at him in the dark, the braggart Big Joe who once was, was long gone. In his place was a scared and frightened boy.

"Big Joe," I said. "It's been a while."

"You put me at risk long enough," Rosanna said to Big Joe. "You're not welcome here anymore." Then she turned to me. "I don't know what you came here for, and I don't know who you are. But I don't want two criminals in my shop. So make it quick, and then I'm asking you to leave without making any trouble." She turned around and went up the stairs.

I turned back to Big Joe. I wasn't prepared to see him in this condition. For the last year and a half, I imagined what our meeting would be like. I planned what I would say and how I would make him pay for killing Irena. But now, standing in the dim light of the back room of Rosanna's ice cream parlor, my anger dissolved. I no longer wanted to kick the crap out of him, and make him suffer any more than he already had.

"How you been?" I asked firmly.

"Okay," he said feebly. "I'm okay." There was a long silence. "How'd you find me?"

"I followed your brother," I said.

Big Joe let out a deep sigh that sounded like it was inside him for years. "He's not the best at keeping secrets, my brother. Or lying low."

"No," I agreed. "Not the best."

There was another long pause. Then Big Joe met my eyes for the first time. "Why did you come here, Davey?"

"I think you know why I'm here, Joe." I said.

"I can take a guess." He said as his face looked down at the floor. "I don't know why you've kept your mouth shut all this time. You didn't owe me nothin'. You could have gotten yourself off the hook and ratted me out, man. Instead you never squealed, and I don't know why."

"Because it was the right thing to do." I said.

"I guess I don't know much about doin' the right thing."

"Now's your time to learn." I said.

He looked up at me expectantly. "What do you mean?" He asked.

"I have a message for you. From Alejandro."

Big Joe looked at me and said, "What's he want?"

"He wants you to pay your debt. And if you don't…he wants blood for blood."

Big Joe swallowed hard. He dealt with Alejandro enough times to know that he wasn't one to joke around.

"And if I don't come clean?" he asked.

"He'll kill your brother," I said.

The news hit him like a freight train. Then he did something I would never have expected in a hundred years. He put his head in his hands and cried.

I wasn't sure what to do, so I put a hand on his shoulder.

"I told him to stay out of that gang," Big Joe said between sobs. "I told him no good would come out of it. It was the only place I could get away from our dad—that's why I was a Wildcat. It was an escape. But I told him he was too smart for that. I told him to get out and go somewhere better. He didn't listen to me."

I nodded, feeling relieved that Big Joe was trusting me with all of this.

"The kid's not cut out for gang life," he continued. "He's not like I was—he's got potential. He's got a future. I just want him to leave before he gets hurt. But if Alejandro's after him…" He choked on his

THE WINDUP

own tears. "Then he's screwed and I can't save him. There's nothing I can do. I can't even save my kid brother."

"Yes, you can," I said softly. "There is something you can do."

Big Joe stopped crying and looked at me. "What?"

"Come clean."

"And fight Alejandro?"

I shook my head. "No. Come clean to the cops."

Big Joe's eyes darkened. He said, "I don't want anything to do with cops. What, are you kidding me?"

I said, "Think about it, Big Joe. If you keep playing Alejandro's game, then the feud between the Rockets and the Wildcats will never end. You really think fighting Alejandro is going to help anything? One of the other Rockets will come after your brother, the minute he turns his back. Connor is determined to prove his worth as a warlord. If you go out and pick a fight with Alejandro, Connor has all the more reason to lead the Wildcats into rumble after rumble. He'll just keep playing the same game...unless you stop it."

"We're not like you," Big Joe said. "I've been reading the papers—Jeannie brings them to me every day. I know all about Olean and you pitching for the Yankees. But I don't have a Major League career in baseball waiting for me. I don't got anything but my gun and my fists. I was born to fight."

"No, Big Joe," I said. "Your father was born to fight. But you can break the pattern. And if you can't do it for yourself...then do it for your brother." I paused for a moment to let my words sink in. "Maybe you're going to have to go to jail so that he doesn't have to...die"

He held back his tears. "You're right," he whispered, his eyes shining. "If I ain't never done nothin' right in my life, this could be the one time I do. Maybe it's my time to do the right thing."

I thought for a moment about how differently this conversation had gone from the way I had expected. I had assumed the way to appeal to Big Joe would be through his anger and jealousy—jealousy of his brother for being warlord of the Wildcats, and personally being angry because he was shut out of his home and neighborhood. But I was wrong. The strongest appeal was through his love and concern for young Connor.

"I have a friend in the force," I said, remembering how instrumental Lieutenant Fabrizi had been in my life. "He's a good guy. I know he will take care of you, especially if I asked him to." I crouched down so that I was at Big Joe's eye level. "Will you tell him the truth about what happened that night?"

Big Joe looked at me with his red-rimmed eyes and nodded.

"Yes," he nodded slowly. "Yes, I will. You also deserve it."

CHAPTER 22
Clearing The Air

By the time I knocked on my parents' door, Mom was already preparing dinner. Frankly, I was totally exhausted. It was one of the longest days of my life—and one I could never have imagined in my wildest dreams, that Big Joe would give himself up. Wow, this was a great accomplishment toward clearing my name. It felt good.

"Duv!" my mother said as she opened the door. "What's wrong? You look exhausted!"

"I am," I admitted.

"Well, why don't you go take a hot bath? It will make you feel better. Dinner will be ready in about an hour. I'm making kosher salami burgers – your favorite."

I smiled. "You're the best, Mom." I kissed her on the cheek before heading straight for a bath.

She was right—the steaming hot water was just what the doctor ordered. I got out feeling refreshed and rejuvenated, ready to tackle the rest of my plan. But there was something I had to do first. I was long overdue for an honest conversation with my folks. It was time.

I got dressed and hurried to the kitchen, where my mother was flipping burgers on the stove.

"Hi, honey," she said. "Dinner's almost ready."

"What can I do to help?" I asked.

She smiled, obviously surprised by the offer. "You can set the table, I guess. Dad will be home shortly."

My Dad came home as I was placing the silverware on the table.

"Hey, Duv," he said. "What a nice surprise to have you home for dinner. What did you do today?"

"You wouldn't believe me if I told you," I said.

"Try me," he replied.

So I told them everything that had happened. My mother shuddered when I got to the part about Alejandro and his knife.

"Oh honey," she said. "I'm so glad you're alright."

"I was unbelievably calm, Mom. I never flinched. I knew if I stayed in control of myself and the situation, that Alejandro would back off."

My Dad shook his head. "I just don't know what the world is coming to. When I was a kid, we didn't play with guns and switchblades. We played with balls and jacks!"

As my Mom kept an eye on the burgers and my Dad poured sodas, I filled them in on finding Big Joe O'Neill. I explained how together we called Lieutenant Fabrizi, who came down from the station himself to get Big Joe's confession and take him in. Before he came, though, Big Joe asked to see Connor. I left the brothers alone so they could say their goodbyes.

Mom and Dad were astonished. "I can't believe it, Duv," my Dad said. "I can't believe he's come forward after all this time."

"To tell you the truth, I think he was relieved," I said. "The guilt has been eating away at him all this time, and it shows. He's like a shell of a human being. First the guilt of killing someone...and then the guilt of lying about it and watching someone else take the blame." I said, "You know, it's funny...and I never thought I'd be saying this...but even Big Joe O'Neill got feelings. He was the meanest guy I knew, and today he was sobbing with his head in his hands. I guess in the end we all have to pay for the choices we make."

I cleared my throat. "Which is kind of what I wanted to talk to you about."

My mother and father looked at each other, then at me.

"What is it, honey?" my mother asked.

"Are you in some kind of trouble?" my father asked.

"No, not at all. Mom, Dad, that's just it—I want to say how sorry I am that you have to ask the question and worry about me getting in some kind of trouble. The trouble I've gotten into so many times, has made it difficult for you to trust me."

I looked at my Dad, trying to find the words for what I wanted to say. "I'm sorry you had to pay for the lawyer, Dad. I'm sorry you had to post bail to get me out of jail. That's something I never wanted you to have to do."

My father looked uncomfortable. "It's okay, Duv," he said quietly. "You don't owe me an apology."

"But I want to give you one. Dad," I said gently, "we need to talk about this, and some other things, in order to clear the air. Okay?"

He continued looking at me. It was difficult to read the expression on his face. "Okay," he finally said, motioning to me with his hand to keep on talking.

I took a deep breath and let it out slowly before continuing. "Life growing up in the South Bronx is hard. You two are the best parents a kid could ask for—please don't misunderstand me. But for years I took you both for granted. I got picked on a lot in elementary school because I was classified as 'a nice little Jewish boy', and I didn't know how to change it. So I looked for comfort—for an escape—and I turned to the streets, where I felt strong and protected. That's where I got involved in a lot of things I shouldn't have."

The saddened look on my Mom's face almost made me stop, I was sure it was upsetting them to hear all of this. But, still, something I was feeling inside encouraged me to continue. "I buried my sadness in alcohol. Even last night, I went out and got drunk, thinking that would numb me to my problems. Mom, I'm sorry you had to see me like that."

She patted my hand softly, unable to speak. At least, I felt she still loved me.

"Last but not least," I went on, bracing myself for the most difficult admission yet, "I turned away from God. I stopped davening. This summer I started again, but before that, I didn't for a long time. I had a huge chip on my shoulder, and I kept challenging God to give me some sign that He was up there. But He didn't. And for a little while, I gave up hope that He was really there, especially after Esther died."

I could see the tears forming in my mother's eyes, the look of consternation on my father's face—but, still, I kept going. I'd gotten this far and I wasn't about to give up now. "Mom, Dad, I've given you both a lot of trouble, and that was selfish on my part. But what I realized today is that we can all make choices, and it's not too late to make a change. I'm not stuck living in the South Bronx or being in a gang. I can choose to leave that behind me...and I have.

"This week has been my worst nightmare. I've been betrayed by so many people—including the guy I thought was my best friend. But after today, I feel more at peace with myself than I ever have. I know who I am, Dave Roth, a pretty good athlete and a decent guy. I'm not a gang member, or a tough guy, or a bad son."

I was getting a little teary myself, and I wiped my eyes. It felt like a huge weight had been lifted from my shoulders. "Mom, Dad, I hope you'll forgive me for everything I've done. I also hope God will forgive me, though I'm still trying to understand Him and His ways. Please, from this day forward, trust me, believe in me, and know that I will never intentionally disappoint either of you ever again."

Without a word, my parents came over to me and we embraced each other.

"We are so proud of you, Duv," my father said, his voice breaking. "It doesn't matter to me if you never pick up a baseball again...we are just so proud to have you as our son."

I felt his love very strongly—more than I ever had before.

"We love you so much, honey," my Mom said. "You are more than forgiven. You are and always will be our loved and precious Duv."

As we moved apart, Mom was so deeply happy, I could see the worry wrinkles on her face disappearing. She held my face in her hands and kissed me, and at that moment, I knew everything would be okay.

My Mom went to the bathroom to fix her makeup, and my Dad and I smiled at one another. I felt closer to him than I had in a long time.

There was a knock on our front door.

Dad said, "Is it the press?" "I swear, Dave, you know I'm not a fighting man...but if those jerks keep messing with my son, they're going to find themselves flat on their backs with their notepads jammed where the sun don't shine!"

It was such an unexpected outburst from my normally quiet and studious father that I couldn't help but laugh. He joined me in laughing as I went to open the door.

When I did, I found Debbie standing by the front door.

"Hiya, stranger!" she said with a grin.

"Hello, Debbie." The image of her stepping in the hotel elevator with Candle flashed across my mind. I had no intention of inviting her into our apartment.

"You missed our lunch date today," she said, with a playful smile. "Why did you stand me up, Davey?"

"That's Dave to you." I was still standing in the doorway. Debbie was a traitor and a liar—had she just come by to rub it in?

She gave me a funny look. "What's wrong? You're acting very strange."

"It's really none of your concern. Have a safe trip back to Olean—thanks for dropping by." Debbie looked hopelessly confused. I was about to close the door when my Mom appeared behind me.

"Is this one of your friends from Olean, Dave?" she said kindly.

"Hi, Mrs. Roth," Debbie said, friendly as ever. "I'm Debbie. It's so nice to meet you."

"It's so nice to meet you!" Mom said. "Dave, why didn't you tell me you met such a lovely girl? Please, Debbie, come in!"

I had no choice but to open the door and let her in. My Mom ushered Debbie into the living room and offered her a cup of tea. Debbie declined. Instead, they chatted about the weather in Olean for a few minutes, and how different life in a small town was from a big city. My Dad came in and joined the conversation, and they both seemed to like Debbie a good deal. I stood silently by, wondering how to politely tell Debbie she was not welcome here. It hurt that she ran around with Candle behind my back, but it made me angry that she had the guts to stand there with my Mom and Dad and act sweet as though nothing had happened.

"Look at me!" my Mom said. "I'm just standing here gabbing away with your friend and hogging her for myself. I'll let you two alone."

My Dad winked at me as they left the room. "Behave yourself, Duv."

Debbie and I stared at each other when they were gone.

"Your parents are lovely, Dave," she said.

"Thanks." There was a tense silence. "Look, Debbie. I have to be honest—I'm not sure why you're here."

"We were supposed to meet for lunch today. Remember?"

"Of course I remember. What I don't remember is where Candle factored into the equation."

"Oh. Then he must have told you." Debbie looked sad. "Gee, I wanted it to be a surprise."

"A surprise?" I shook my head in disbelief. "Some surprise." I said.

She looked at me intently. "Are we talking about the same thing?" She asked.

I answered, "I don't know—you tell me. Were you at the hotel yesterday?"

"Yes, I was. After the game." She said.

"You were there with Candle." I said.

She answered, "That's right. I had to ask Candle for his help. He had something I needed." She paused. "How did you know?"

"Because I saw you get in the elevator with him."

Debbie's eyes got very big. Her deductive reasoning skills were kicking into high gear again. "And you thought I…"

I cut her off. "It doesn't matter what I thought. Look, if you liked my best friend all this time, I just wish you had told me the truth instead of letting me think you actually liked me."

Debbie said, "Oh, Dave. No wonder you didn't want to meet me for lunch. You really think that's the kind of girl I am?"

I shrugged. "I don't know. I guess I don't know you well enough to know what kind of girl you are."

"Well believe me: I'm not that kind. Do you know why I went up to Candle's room?" She asked.

I shook my head.

"I went up there to ask Candle if he would help me…help you."

"What?" I wasn't following Debbie's line of thought.

She pulled something out of her pocket that was wrapped in a brown paper bag. Then she shook it out of the bag until it was resting in her palm. It was a black rectangle, about eight by four inches, with a red dial in the middle.

"Do you know what this is?" she asked.

"No."

"It's a tape recorder." She answered.

I gave it a closer look. "I've never seen one so small before."

"That's because they've never made them this small before," Debbie said proudly. "It's the Mohawk Midget Recorder—the first battery-operated pocket tape recorder in the world."

"There's actually a tape in there?" I asked.

"Uh huh." She handed me the recorder and I marveled at how small and light it was. It probably weighed less than a pound.

"How did you find out about it?" I asked.

"I told you—I love detective stories. I get all the magazines. *Ellery Queen's Mystery Magazine. Headline Detective.* And the Mohawk is the hottest new thing in the world of private eyes. I figured if you could get Big Joe's confession on tape, then you would have a bulletproof defense. You could submit the tape anonymously to the police and they'd know who the killer was—and you wouldn't have to go on record for ratting Big Joe out."

"Wow, Debbie. You really thought this through." I ran my fingers nimbly across the recorder. "Is it expensive?"

"It cost $249.50." She answered.

I nearly choked. "Wow, that's a lot of money."

"Exactly. And unfortunately, I don't have ready access to that kind of cash. I knew a shop in the city that sold them, but it was way out of my price range." She said.

"So you went to ask Candle for help," I said, finally putting the pieces together.

"That's right. I knew that Candle's family had money, and I knew he would be willing to help me if it meant clearing your name. As it turned out, we didn't even have to ask his family. He was so eager to help that he offered to use the five-hundred-dollar check you guys got as a bonus from the Yankees. So I had more than enough money to buy the Mohawk and the shoulder harness that goes under your suit."

She smiled at me. "Candle loves you like a brother, Dave. He'd do anything to help you."

I couldn't believe it. I felt terrible, that I accused my best friend and Debbie, of betraying me when in reality, they were only working together to help me…Wow, I blew that one!

"Debbie," I said quietly, "I feel awful. Please forgive me for jumping to the wrong conclusion. I just saw you with him at the hotel, and I got so jealous and angry…I should have trusted you both."

"It's okay. You've had a hard week. I don't blame you for not knowing whom you can trust." She picked up the Mohawk and cradled it in her palm. "So what do you think about my idea? Should we go back to the ice cream parlour and get Big Joe to spill the beans?"

"Actually," I said with a big grin, "I've got some good news for you, too."

I took Debbie's hands in mine and told her all about my day. By the end of the story, she was crying happy tears.

"So he confessed everything," she said. "Wow. I can't believe it. You're something else, Dave." She looked at me admiringly.

"I think it was being in the right place at the right time," I said. "And taking action. That's what I realized when I was staring at Alejandro's knife today, that it's time I take control of my own destiny. I've got to take responsibility for my own life."

She looked at me with her big green eyes. "I'm glad you weren't hurt, Dave. I don't know what I'd do without you."

I leaned in to kiss her, and her lips felt and tasted amazing. It seemed like every kiss with Debbie was more spectacular, each time.

"So what now?" Debbie asked. She put the Mohawk on the table. "I guess you won't be needing this after all." She looked a little disappointed.

"Actually, I do." I pulled her in for a hug. "Debbie, you're brilliant, you know that? Because this is exactly what I need for part two of my plan."

"Really?" She looked pleased. "I'm so glad!"

"Me, too. And there's one person who can help us." I rubbed my hands together, delighted by how perfectly the plan was lining up in my head. "I'm going to give Sandy Abrams a call." I said.

Debbie's face darkened as she pulled away from me and said, "Isn't that the girl who wrote the article in *Look*? Why on earth would you want to talk to her?"

"Because I think she can help us. And I think she'll want to."

I reached for the phone my parents kept by the sofa. Debbie put her hand over mine.

"Dave," she said quietly. "Can I ask you something personal?"

I shrugged my shoulders. "Shoot."

"Do you like Sandy?" She asked.

Man, I wasn't expecting that! I felt my face getting hot, but tried to keep my emotions under control. "Why do you ask?" I calmly queried her.

"I'd just like to know."

I looked at her for a long time, trying to decide what the right answer was. Finally, I thought the right answer was the truth.

"Well, Debbie, I did." I said.

She nodded. "Okay. Thank you for telling me the truth."

"Are you upset?" I asked.

She smiled. "Well, sure, a little. Wouldn't you be jealous if it were the other way around?" I didn't have to think about it long—the thought of Debbie with Candle had made me a little crazy. I nodded vigorously, which made her smile again.

"Do you still have feelings for her?" she asked.

"Are you kidding?" I said. "Hell, no! Not after what she did. And even before that, I wasn't crazy about her. She's obviously attractive, but I find her too aggressive. She's pushy and overly sure of herself. Whatever was going on between us was very superficial. But you, Debbie..." I brushed the hair out of her eyes. "You're something special. I have fun just being with you. I think you're sweet and sexy at the same time. And damn, you're beautiful. I feel comfortable with you... and like you're willing to take it one day at a time."

She kissed me softly on the mouth. "I am, Dave. I am."

"To be honest, Deb...I really care about you."

I could see how happy this made her—she blushed again, and I loved it. "I care about you, too," she said.

I leaned in for another kiss, but she turned her head so I caught her cheek instead. "Uh uh uh," she said, shaking her finger playfully in my face. "We've got business to attend to. If you say we need Sandy on our team, that's fine with me. I trust you. But one request, Dave?"

"Anything." I answered.

"Let's call her together." She said.

"It's a deal. And when this is all over, I'd like to take you out on a real date—to a drive-in movie. Okay?" I asked.

"That's a deal," Debbie said, very pleased.

"Hey kids!" Mom said, popping her head around the corner. "Debbie, we would love you to stay for dinner."

"I'd love to," Debbie said happily.

"Those salami burgers smell great, Mom," I said. "I'm going to need lots of energy for tomorrow."

"Tomorrow?" She looked confused. "Why, honey? Where are you going?"

I stood and stretched as a big smile spread across my face.

"To the Yankee Stadium. There's someone I need to see."

CHAPTER 23

Straight To The Top

The next day, the morning sun was beating down on the streets of the South Bronx. It was hot. I climbed the steps to the glass office on top of the Yankee Stadium. I was done messing around—it was time to go straight to the top. And the envelope under my arm gave me a legitimate reason to.

I knocked on Martin Fletcher's door. When I got no response, I knocked harder.

"I'm coming, for chrissakes," said a gruff voice from inside. The door swung open. "Who the hell are you?"

"I'm Dave Roth. You hired me to pitch for the Yankees, remember?" I stepped inside the office, even though Fletcher hadn't invited me in.

"I know your name. Who the hell do you think you are coming up to my office unannounced like this? I'm a very busy man."

I turned and looked him in the eye and said, "I figured it was high time you and I had a little chat."

Fletcher was still standing at the doorway, glaring at me. "You've got a lot of nerve, kid." He said.

I answered, "I could say the same for you, sir, you've got a lot of damn nerve."

I couldn't believe the words that were coming out of my mouth. It was like someone else had taken control of my body, and there I was, challenging the GM of the New York Yankees.

Frankly, it felt great.

"You plan on telling me why you barged into my office, Roth?"

I answered, "As soon as you tell me why you're dead set on destroying my reputation and killing my career with the Yankees."

The Ballplayer

Fletcher was fuming. I could tell he was trying to appear unflustered, but he was furious at this breach of protocol.

He said, "I don't know what the hell you're talking about. Are you trying to tell me that your bad choices from over a year ago are somehow my fault? That I set it up for you to kill that girl? Sorry to disappoint you kid, but I don't really give a damn about your private affairs before you played for us. But the minute we added you to the big club's roster? It became my concern."

I took a deep breath and said, "First of all, I didn't kill anyone." I slid the envelope across the desk. "Take a look at that."

"What's this?" Fletcher yelled as he pulled the papers out of the envelope and scanned the first page. He flipped angrily through a few more. "What is it?"

"That, sir," I said "is the confession of the man who killed Irena Rosario the night of April 29, 1952. He gave himself up to the police yesterday."

Fletcher stared at me. "What are you saying?"

"I'm saying that I didn't kill Irena, and now there's proof. The official copy is on file at the 42nd Precinct, the local police station with Lieutenant Fabrizi, the detective presiding over the case. But I thought you might like to see a copy." He shoved the papers back across the desk toward me, but I shook my head. "Keep them." I continued. "I've already made arrangements with the press—they'll be printing the true version of events in tomorrow's papers."

"So you think it's really that easy?" Fletcher asked, his voice very angry and mean. "Someone else fired the gun and you're off the hook? Grow up, kid. You were a gang warlord! You're not worthy of wearing Yankee pinstripes!" He continued, "A crazy warlord! You fought with knives and bats and brass knuckles. You're a criminal, and I don't care how many spics you did or didn't kill—you don't deserve a spot on a Major League baseball team. And especially not on this one."

I took a deep breath and said, "I'm not saying I'm proud of my behavior. I was the leader of a street gang—whoever did your dirty work got that part right. But I left the gang and haven't looked back. I challenge you to dig up the back stories on any one of your players—half of those guys were involved in gangs in Harlem, Brooklyn and the Bronx when they were teenagers. They stole stuff and got in fights and ended up in a police station drunk on more than one occasion. It's a double standard, Fletcher, and you know it."

If looks could kill, Fletcher would have shot me that minute.

"Make your point, Roth." He said.

"My point is that you're a bigot and a racist."

"Excuse me?" he asked, furious.

I said, "You heard me. I said you're a bigot and a racist. Your bigotry has kept the Yankees from getting some great talent. If you want the Yankees to forever be an all-white team, and if you want to keep your boys all a bunch of WASPs, you're doing a great job. But times are changing, Fletcher. You're the GM of a great team. America's best team, in my opinion, however, the Yankees are going to flounder and die if you don't wake up."

"So the Yankees are going to flounder and die without you," Fletcher sneered.

"Hardly. I'm one guy. I'm nobody. Actually, thanks to you, I'm on the cover of every paper from here to Buffalo, so I guess I am somebody...but not the somebody I really am. My point is that you don't actually care about all this other crap you pretend to. The only thing you really care about is my heritage."

"Meaning?" He asked.

"The fact that I'm a Jew." I answered.

The room was so silent I could hear the faint buzz of the floor lamp.

Furiously he said through clenched teeth, "Are you accusing the Yankees of being an anti-Semitic organization?"

I answered, "No, sir. The Yankees are fine. I'm accusing you of being an Anti-Semite."

Suddenly, Fletcher was just two inches away from me—surprisingly quick for an old guy. He had me by the collar, and his face was so close to mine I could see his nose hairs. His breath reeked of cigar smoke and booze.

"You've got a lot of balls," he began, "a lot of big balls to come in here and confront me like this. But let me tell you something, Roth."

He gripped my collar tighter, so tight that it hurt my neck. "You were nobody before, and you're nobody now. You're a punk Jew from the ghetto with immigrant parents who foul up the streets of my city. Got that?"

I answered with a low and calm voice, much like when Alejandro threatened me. "Is that why you got Abrams to print a front-page story…that amounts to libel?"

He laughed in my face. "You must think you're real clever. Did a little detective work and now you've got it all figured out, right? You don't know how it works in the big leagues, Roth. Abrams is a pawn in my hand. I've got him wrapped around my little finger. Politicians are easy—they'll do anything for the right reasons. All you have to do is apply a little pressure in the right spot."

"So you make a generous campaign donation and he prints up the dirt. What a perfect partnership. Did you know he was a Jew, too? Your own kind betrayed you?" He said.

Fletcher's eyes narrowed as he continued, "You Jews make great businessmen. You would do anything for a few extra bucks. But the Yankees are a classy team and you don't belong here. You belong on the streets with the rest of the kikes and niggers."

"Give me one game to prove how wrong you are." I answered.

He laughed again. "Your people dirty up the diamond, Roth."

"One game," I said. "And if I blow it, you'll never see me again."

He took a step backwards and sized me up. It became obvious to me, although he hated me…he couldn't help admire my guts.

"You don't know who you're messing with, Roth," he said. "You're playing in the big leagues now."

"Wrong," I said, enjoying the freedom that came from saying whatever I wanted. "I'll be playing in the big leagues when you give me a chance to."

He folded his arms across his chest.

"You've got more balls than McPherson and Stengel put together, I'll give you that," he said, shaking his head. "Roth, you're an idiot. You're a rookie who doesn't know when to stop. Sure, you've got one hell of a throwing arm…in the little leagues. When it comes to Major

League baseball? I'm not sure you can take the heat."

"I do well under pressure," I said. "Look at how I'm handling dealing with a creep like you. If I had a chance to prove myself on the diamond, you would see that it's not a problem."

He deliberated for a moment that seemed to go on for eternity. "Alright." Fletcher said.

"Alright...what?" Dave asked.

Fletcher shrugged. "You've got your game, kid. I'll talk to the papers and get them to low-key the gang stuff. But you better kick some Red Sox butt, or I'll personally see to it that you'll never get a shot with any organization anywhere on this planet."

I wasn't stupid—there was definitely a threat in Fletcher's deal. I knew he would keep his word. But there was also an opportunity. Call me crazy, but I'll take the opportunity any time.

"Agreed," I said.

"Good. Now get the hell out of here," he said, "and get down to the field. You're back on the roster for tomorrow's game."

I swallowed. "Against the Red Sox?"

"That's right. And you better be ready."

Back on the street, I took a moment to catch my breath. I hadn't realized how fast my heart had been beating during my confrontation with Fletcher, but now that I was out of his office, the insanity of what I had just done hit me full force.

"Dave!" Debbie ran up to meet me. She'd been hanging out in the diner on E. 161st Street, waiting for me. "Did you get it?"

"He said everything I expected him to say," I said, "and a whole lot more." I reached into my jacket and pulled the Mohawk Midget Recorder out of the shoulder holster. "And it's all right here."

Debbie clapped her hands together in delight. "We did it!"

The ploy had worked, catch Fletcher by complete surprise, and make him so angry that he spilled all his hatred and showed his true colors. And now we had him on tape confessing his underhanded dealings with Abrams...not to mention his bigotry.

"We did. And get this, Debbie—he agreed to let me play in tomorrow's game against the Red Sox."

"No kidding!" She thought about this for a moment then said, "I guess we won't need to use the tape for blackmail after all. Looks like your diplomatic skills have saved the day again. Maybe you should go into politics," she teased.

"Ha. Not in this lifetime! But I have a feeling that tape's going to come in handy as collateral. Never know when we might need it. Are we still set to meet with Sandy?"

Debbie nodded and said, "She's coming to the soda shop this afternoon. And we've got all sorts of goodies for her when she does—Big Joe's confession, and a tape exposing Martin Fletcher. We've practically written her next cover story for her!" She smiled. "She couldn't apologize enough on the phone about the *Look* feature. I think she got pressured into doing something she didn't want to do."

"That's my feeling, too. She's really not a bad girl." I said.

Debbie raised her eyebrows.

"But she's nowhere near as good a girl as you!" I added, and stole a quick kiss.

"Dave Roth!" Debbie said, after a long kiss. "Why are you still hanging around with me? Don't you have a game to play tomorrow?"

"Yes, I guess I do! I better head to the clubhouse right away."

She handed me a bag with my baseball stuff. "Thought you might need this."

"Debbie, you're the greatest!" I said hugging her before grabbing the bag and running back toward the stadium.

"You're the greatest, Dave," she called after me. "Now go make us all proud!"

CHAPTER 24

The Big Game – The Show

By eleven the next morning, Yankee Stadium was filled to capacity. Over 50,000 people were there as the Red Sox took the field for their pre-game warm-ups. I saw Ted Williams and the rest of the Sox, stretching, running, hitting fungo, or taking BP. Suddenly, it all seemed very real.

I was about to play baseball with a Major League team and pitch for the New York Yankees. Wow, is this a dream?

All the guys were wonderful, accepting me back on the team with no questions asked. I had a feeling Eddie Lopat had something to do with that.

"We're glad you're back, Dave," Eddie said to me the day before. "By the way, that Hare is a real jerk. Who does he think he his?"

Hare had been practicing with the Yankees for the last couple of days, and I imagined that was plenty of time for him to make more than a few enemies.

"Tell me about it," I said. "I'm glad to be back."

Casey told Hare he could sit in the dugout and watch the game, but he got so mad when they told him he wasn't pitching, he stormed out of the clubhouse and left. No one has seen him since, and no one seems to care.

While I was warming up, I realized the opportunity I dreamed about my whole life was about to happen. I worked hard for this chance, and when it looked like they were going to take it all away from me, I fought to get it back. I've never been prouder to be exactly who I was—a Jewish former gang warlord, a guy named Dave Roth who knew how to throw a baseball, and one lucky dude!

I heard a faint chant in the stands. At first I thought my ears were playing tricks on me, but it gradually grew louder until it was unmistakable: "Davey! Davey! Davey!" I looked up to see my parents and Debbie in the stands, cheering with all their might. It made my heart swell.

But it wasn't just them—it was the people all around them. It was people who didn't know me and whom I didn't know, but who were yelling my name all the same. It was an amazing feeling. They must have read the papers this morning, I thought. Everybody loves the story of the underdog—especially when the underdog was wrongfully accused.

Sandy did a brilliant job delivering the news to the press. She'd told Debbie and me that she would never write for *Look* again—but that didn't mean she wasn't going to be a top-notch journalist. She had stayed up all night writing a dynamite piece of investigative journalism that cleared my name beyond a shadow of a doubt, and the *New York Herald-Tribune* had printed it on the front page this morning. She was saving the good stuff on Fletcher for a piece she planned to sell to *Time* magazine.

"Who needs *Look*?" she said to us the day before, as we all sipped root beer floats at the diner on East 161st Street.

"I'll handle the press," Sandy had assured us. "All you have to do, Dave, is kick some butt on that field."

And that's exactly what I planned to do.

I felt loose as I threw my warm-up pitches. Then I headed into the clubhouse to do what was arguably the most important thing, I prayed. Prayer to me was like meditating—very calming and grounding. When I was through, I was ready to give it my best shot.

"I'll be in the dugout for the whole game, Dave," Eddie Lopat assured me. "Any time you need me, I'll be right there, just give me a look."

"Thanks, Eddie," I said, very grateful for his support. Lopat was my hero, my mentor and my teacher—a pitcher whose nickname of "Steady Eddie" was well-deserved. I hoped that some of his steadiness had rubbed off on me during all the time we spent together. Right then, I needed it.

The Big Game — The Show

It was time for the game of a lifetime. My destiny was about to unfold.

Bob Sheppard, the public announcer for the Yankees, started his announcement: "Ladies and gentlemen, welcome to Yankee Stadium, the home of champions. Today the Yankees will be playing the Boston Red Sox in the race for the pennant. With a Yankee win today they could clinch the 1953 American League Pennant! Sheppard announced the names of the visiting Red Sox starting lineup--Joe Umphlett, George Kell, Casey White, Jimmy Piersall, Milt Bolling, Hal Brown, Ike DeLock, Dick Gernert, and of course, Ted Williams. What an incredible lineup.

"Starting for the New York Yankees, playing shortstop and leading off—Phil Rizzuto." Wild applause greeted each successive name. Batting second, Billy Martin, second base. Batting third, Mickey Mantle, at center field."

"Mickey! Mickey! Mickey!" fans chanted. He was a huge crowd favorite.

Sheppard continued with the line-up: Hank Bauer, left field, was fourth; Yogi Berra, catching, was fifth. Sixth was Gene Woodling, right field, and seventh was Joe Collins, first base. Gil McDougald, third base, was eighth; and batting ninth and pitching, now warming up in front of the Yankees dugout, was Dave Roth.

Me...Wow!...Unreal!

"Folks," Sheppard said, "Dave Roth has just been brought up from our Minor League team, the Olean Yankees. Let's give him a big welcome." The cheers and screams were deafening.

The Yankees took the field. And I was officially a Yankee, if only for a day, up for the proverbial cup of coffee up from the Minors. If I pitched well today, I could stick. Just throw strikes, I thought. Don't get overwhelmed, even though the view from the mound was suddenly overwhelming. The fans were yelling like crazy and I could hear individual voices through the crowd yelling "Go get 'em, kid!" and

"Beat the Sox!"

Man, I thought. These New York fans are great!

Then the home plate umpire, Art Passerelli, yelled out, "Play ball!"—and the battle began.

I couldn't wait to get my hands on a ball. When I held it, I felt the stitches under my thumb and centered myself. My moment had finally come. I wasn't pitching to prove myself to Fletcher or my parents or anyone else in the stadium that day. I was pitching because I loved this game, and because I wanted to be right there, on the pitcher's mound, more than anywhere else in the world.

Okay, Red Sox, I thought to myself. Let's see what you got.

Leading off for the Sox was Joe Umphlett. He was a dangerous .290 hitter, but I didn't give him the chance, strike one, strike two, strike three. He just watched three curveballs fall off the table.

Hitting second, from the left side, was George Kell, who'd hit .300 during the season. Bang! Into Yogi's glove—strike one, strike two, strike three, and the Yankees had two outs. Holy cow, three straight off-the-table curveballs again.

Hitting third, from the left side, was catcher Casey White, who was a star. But even White was no match for the curveballs I was throwing. He didn't even swing at the first pitch, the second and third time he tried but couldn't catch up to it. Three strikes and we had our third out. The fans gave me a standing ovation.

In the bottom of the first inning, our leadoff batter stepped in—Phil Rizzuto, who worked the count to 2-2. Hard-throwing pitcher Ike DeLock threw a sharp curveball, and Rizzuto hit it high and deep to centerfield. Piersall was under it. One out.

Billy Martin was up next. He took a quick strike then ball one. Next pitch, he hit a line shot right through the middle that almost took DeLock's head off. The shortstop made a great play. Two out.

Mantle was next. The crowds went wild when he stepped up to the plate. Hitting lefty, he was trying to lay down a perfect bunt on the

The Big Game — The Show

first pitch, but he popped it up foul. White caught it. Three out.

I headed back to the mound. I was on the warpath. This was a different kind of warpath than I'd ever been on before. Still in my zone, I barely heard the fans rocking the stadium. All I could think of was winning that game.

It was the top of the second inning. No score.

"We've got ourselves a ball game!" Rizzuto said, as he passed me on the way to his position.

Did we ever, I thought.

Hitting fourth for the Red Sox, from the right side, was Jimmy Piersall. I fired a fastball at him—high and on the outside part of the plate—for strike one. Man, that must have been a hundred-mile-an-hour fastball!

Strike two was another fastball, low and inside. Then bang! Into Yogi's glove—strike three for the first out.

With one out, Milt Bolling was hitting fifth, from the right side. Bolling was an excellent contact hitter, but he fouled back my fastball for strike one. Finally, someone had swung the bat and hit something!

A fastball again, and another foul ball—strike two. Then, bang! Right into Yogi's glove, high and tight, strike three.

Coming up with two outs in the top of the second, Ted Williams was sixth in the Red Sox lineup. He had a lifetime .410 batting average and was renowned for his intimidating look. There he was in the flesh, back from serving as a Lieutenant Marine Corps pilot in Korea. They called him "The Thumper" because of his spectacular skills as a hitter. He was an MVP and a player I always respected immensely... even if he played for the other guys. Maybe I should have been intimidated, pitching to probably the greatest hitter of all time, but I was in my zone, just staring at Yogi's mitt. The fans were cheering so loud, I couldn't hear the umpire's call. Williams swung once, but it went foul. Next pitch was a blazer—strike two. I was nervous. Was I going to be able to pull off striking him out? I kept on staring at Yogi and bang! Strike three, three outs.

"Unbelievable!" our manager, Casey Stengel, shouted. "Eighteen pitches, six strikeouts! This kid's on fire!"

We took the field. It was the bottom of the second. I went to my corner of the dugout and waved Yogi over to sit by me. I wanted to talk about curveballs versus fastballs for the third inning.

"Dave," Yogi said, in his patient way, "I'm up this inning. Got to think about hitting for a minute."

I nodded. "Sure thing. DeLock's got a mean fastball," I agreed. "You know what? I think that's what I'll throw, too, next inning. All fastballs. How about it?"

Yogi looked at me with admiration.

"They weren't kidding about you," he said. "You're somethin' else, kid."

I grinned. The game was turning into a real battle—a serious pitcher's duel!

CHAPTER 25

Top Of The Ninth

I threw all strikes in the third, and retired the side in order. As the game wore on, it was a classic pitchers' duel. Hits were scarce, runs were nonexistent, and not a batter on either side reached second base. DeLock had pitched brilliantly, but by the seventh inning he was showing signs of tiring. So, Sox manager Lou Boudreau brought reliever Hal Brown in. Hal was living up to his reputation as a knuckleballer with outstanding control. We weren't hitting the Red Sox' pitchers any more than they were hitting me.

But I could proudly say that I was a match for the best the Red Sox could throw at us. There I was, Dave Roth, the Minor League pitcher who somehow earned a spot on the New York Yankees...and I was holding my own. Casey left me in for the first eight innings and wasn't warming up a reliever to come in for me. It was the top of the ninth. In my mind he had no reason to, I was pitching a shutout. I wasn't tired. On the contrary, I felt like I could go on forever. The feeling was totally unreal.

I glanced up at the stadium clock. It was 2:05 p.m. The game had flown by. Still no score.

The fans went from frenzied cheering and screaming to attentive silence. The tension was so thick you could slice it with a knife, but somehow it didn't affect me at all. When I dared to glance at the stands, I saw every fan in the ballpark standing and watching me, probably to see if I still had what it took to get through the next half inning. Did Casey know what he was doing, leaving me in to handle this kind of pressure? Every pitch could mean clinching the pennant. But like I told Fletcher, I didn't fold under pressure. Far from it—I was smooth as butter and cool as ice.

As I stood on the pitcher's mound, the realization hit me—that the pennant may hinge on what happened next. The crowd wanted me to throw a complete game shut out. But could I do it? After everything I had been through…did I have the energy to do what I came here to do? Or was I just kidding myself?

I stood, staring at the ball in my hand, unable to move. Suddenly, the weight of it all fell on my shoulders, paralyzing me.

After what seemed like hours, the rest of the guys sensed that something was wrong. Casey told Lopat to go out to the mound and talk to me.

"You okay?" Lopat asked.

I shook my head. "This is all a dream, Eddie," I said quietly. "It's gotta be a dream. It's too strange to think it's not. I'm gonna wake up soon, so who cares?"

Lopat stared at me and asked again, "Are you okay, kid?"

Everything became a little blurry. The fans in their seats were silent, moving in slow motion. This wasn't real. None of it had been real, not the no-hit game I pitched…not meeting Debbie. Olean had never existed. Neither had the Team of Destiny. I was home in New York, all right, but not pitching at Yankee Stadium. I was back in the jail in the South Bronx, paying for a crime I didn't commit. I felt a little woozy, then all of a sudden, I heard Eddie's voice say, "It's not a dream, Dave."

"I'm okay," I quickly assured him, snapping out of my trance.

"We're counting on you," Lopat said. "Don't quit on us now. Just visualize the strike zones, like I showed you all those months ago." Then he put a hand on my shoulder. "I know who you are, Dave," he added. "Just be yourself and all will be well…This is real."

Suddenly, everything snapped into focus. I smiled, inspired, brought back to reality by Lopat's words.

"I don't know what came over me," I said, "but I'm okay now."

Lopat swatted my behind with his hand, gave me a wink, and headed back to the dugout.

Hal Brown, Boston's star reliever, came to bat. I thought for a moment about whether it made sense strategically for the Red Sox not to bat for him. I guess they didn't have any faith in the rest of their bullpen and wanted to keep Hal around for the bottom of the ninth.

I went into my full windup and threw. Brown showed bunt, but it didn't matter. Strike one—that fastball was easily over a hundred miles per hour! I followed it with strike two, which he stabbed at and missed...wasted a pitch low and outside to see if he'd go for it...and then fired a fastball over the outside corner. He froze and watched it go by for strike three. He was as dejected as the crowd was elated. It was getting so loud in the Stadium I could barely hear myself think.

Dick Gernert stepped in next, dug his back foot into the dirt, and tried to stare me down. Sorry, Dick. I've seen tougher than you on a street corner in the South Bronx at midnight. Maybe having been a warlord in my previous life was an advantage on the pitcher's mound!

Gernert took a quick strike one, a curveball that dropped off the table. Then, strike two, as he, too, tried to bunt and missed by a mile. Then, strike three, two out. Just like that.

The Yankee dugout was going nuts, and so were the fans. But I stayed focused on my mission. This was a war, and I was paced for action.

Jimmy Piersall came up next. He smiled at me, as if to say, good game, kid. I wondered if he was trying to break my concentration.

Yogi Berra ran out to talk to me.

"Hey, Davey," Yogi said. "Holy-moly, you are the real deal! I didn't know what to believe before, what with the bad press and all, but I'm not wondering anymore. Don't let Piersall break your concentration. Sure, the guy's a great ballplayer...but so are you, meat! And remember, kid, it ain't over 'til it's over!"

"It ain't over until I retire Piersall!" I told myself.

I fired a fastball for strike one. That one had to be clocked at a hundred and five, at least. It froze Piersall in his tracks, that much I knew. He sure wasn't smiling anymore.

Next, I threw a curveball, off the table. Piersall swung and missed by more than a mile. Usually I work really quickly, just lean in, get the sign, and fire the pill. But this time, I wanted him to think about what had just happened.. I wanted it to prey on his mind for a couple of moments before I looked in for the sign.

The Ballplayer

I wound up, threw—and strike three! A fastball that hit Yogi's glove with the sound of a truck smashing into a wall!

It was the third out. I couldn't believe it.

I held the Red Sox scoreless for nine straight innings. I kept my head down. I didn't want to look like I was gloating as I saw Piersall throw his bat toward the dugout with a look of disgust and disappointment on his face.

It was the bottom of the ninth, score, nothing, nothing. I knew that if we didn't get a run this inning, Casey would never run me out there for the top of the tenth. He would play the percentages and bring in a fresh arm. And I couldn't blame him if he did that. I glanced at the lineup on the scoreboard in center field. I was fourth up. If anybody got on, I'd come to bat. Unless Casey took the bat out of my hands for a pinch hitter. Why shouldn't he, if it came to that? Plenty of power on the Yankees' bench. I tried to put all thoughts of hitting out of my mind and instead began to visualize myself coming out, against all odds, to pitch the tenth if we didn't score.

Berra led off and negotiated a five pitch walk, while one of the best home run hitters, Joe Collins, twirled three bats in the on deck circle. Maybe Brown will make a mistake. Collins came up and everybody in the Stadium were on their feet, yelling to Joe to just park one in the short right field porch and end the game…and clinch the pennant for us. You could tell from Collins' stance that he was thinking the same thing. He just wanted to rip one.

Maybe he wanted it a little too much. He waited too long to turn on the only fastball he saw, fouled it off down the right field line, and then hit a slow grounder to the third baseman on the next pitch. The crowd fell silent.

One out, man on second.

Gil McDougald stepped up to the plate. "Gil! Gil! Gil!", the fans were screaming. I took my place in the on deck circle, almost too nervous to swing the bats.

Brown knocked Gil down on the first pitch, which brought everyone in the Yankee dugout to their feet. Did he do it on purpose? Hard to say. Gil was okay. He stepped in and—oh, my God, I couldn't believe it! He went down again! Brown was worse than Hare. By now, the Yankees were all on the top step of the dugout, angry as hell, ready to charge the mound. But Gil just got up, dusted off his uniform, and stepped in again. A pro's pro.

Next, Hal hung a curve, but Gil couldn't do anything with it. He swung feebly and popped it up. Two down.

And then, just like that, I was up. My last at-bat in my first Major League game. I glanced into the dugout at Casey, to see if he was looking around the dugout for someone to grab a bat and replace me. But no—he was just sitting there impassively, eyes half-shut, as if he were about to catch a nap instead of trying to manage the Yankees back to the World Series. No pinch hitter. And no reliever was warming up. I guess Case thought I'd either win the game with a swing of the bat or go back out there and face the Sox in the tenth. His confidence in me tripled the confidence I had in myself.

Before I left two of my bats on the on-deck circle, I glanced at Eddie. He winked and shouted, "Just be you."

No score. Two outs and Yogi dancing off second. Ball one—had to duck on that one. It was close! Because Brown had excellent control, I guessed that he was giving me a message—one that I got, no problem.

Next pitch, a called strike right over the middle of the plate—a great pitch to hit. Okay, I thought. I've got you now. That's it—go to your mouth with your fingers and put that curveball out there where I like it. Okay, Dave, not too anxious, watch the ball, visualize…

BAM! It was a rocket. It was high, it was far, and it was gone—landing somewhere in the right-field upper-deck seats. A two-run homer. My first Major League hit… a home run! The game was over!

I was in shock as I rounded the bases, not too fast, not too slow. I was keeping my head down—I didn't want anyone to think I was show boating. The hardest thing was not to grin. Or go crazy. I just concentrated on touching every base—I didn't want an appeal play. When I got to home plate, the whole team mobbed me. I thought I was going to pass out from excitement.

The fans were out of control! When I got to the dugout, they just kept cheering—wanting me to take a curtain call. Eddie pushed me to get back on the field, but I was reluctant. All that attention made me kind of shy.

But it was what the fans wanted, so I stepped out, tipped my cap, and smiled. I waved to my folks and Debbie who were sitting behind the home plate screens, and they waved back. They were beaming.

We had won, 2-0.

The fans went wild. The team ran out to mob me, like we just won the World Series. In my mind, we kind of did.

"Yankees! Yankees! Yankees!" came the chanting from the stands.

I could do nothing but fall to my knees and thank God, as tears streamed down my face.

I did it.

No, I realized. We did it.

My teammates lifted me on their shoulders and held me high in their embrace. I couldn't help but look up and into the glass office at the top of the Yankee Stadium. Was that Martin Fletcher leaning against the glass, smoking a cigar? Maybe I was imagining things…but even from all the way down on the diamond, I could have sworn I saw a mix of awe and respect in his eyes.

CHAPTER 26

A Happy Ending

The clubhouse scene was wild—everyone was laughing, crying and hugging each other.

I got a lot more congratulations from the team, which was great. I really felt like I'd made them proud. After having my name dragged through the mud for the last week, it felt like they were ready to put the past—my past—behind them. And so was I.

Eddie told me that Casey wanted to see me in his office right away, so I hustled over, hoping nothing was wrong.

"Congratulations, Davey," Casey said as I closed the door behind me. "You've got a big-time future in baseball, and with the New York Yankees. You did a great job out there today." Then he looked at me. "Now, Eddie said something about this dream you were talking about out on the mound. What's all that about?"

"Well," I answered, "I had it fixed in my head it was all a dream. Nothing can be this good. It wasn't that long ago that I was in jail for a murder I didn't commit. Before that, I was just some troublemaker hanging out with a gang on the streets of the South Bronx. No one ever heard of Dave Roth. And it was only a few days ago, I was at the lowest point in my life. I was dragged through the dirt by the higher ups and thought I would never be able to climb out of the mud."

Casey was thinking. From the look on his face, I had a feeling he knew who was to blame.

"It doesn't matter now," I assured him. "I can take care of myself, and I took care of it. But the fact is that today, I pitched for the New York Yankees against the Red Sox. It's unreal! The season in Olean, the Team of Destiny, making so many friends…then the grand slam—being brought up to the parent club. I'm playing for the New York Yankees! Mr. Stengel, tell me that's not a dream!"

Casey nodded but said nothing, waiting for me to continue.

"I'm sorry I got so unfocused," I told him. "I guess I was afraid of waking up, my head was somewhere else…maybe back in apartment 1D at 660 Southern Boulevard, in the South Bronx."

I took a deep breath and added, "It won't happen again—but if you want to get rid of me, I'll understand. I'm so happy to have played today's game that if I never play another game again, I'll die happy."

Casey laughed. "Are you crazy? You're not going anywhere! Our new star pitcher is going to help us win a World Series."

I laughed, too, out of relief and said, "Eddie was the one who woke me up when he said it wasn't a dream. I know if he says it, it has to be true. I'm thrilled this is all really happening. And I want to thank you for keeping me—I won't disappoint you."

Casey gave me his famous crooked grin. "I know you won't. Now go have a good dinner with the guys," he said. "I'm happy you're here. And I'll tell you a secret. Howie told me he's gonna fire Fletcher and give you your five hundred dollar bonus check tomorrow."

"Holy cow!" I said.

"Don't tell anybody you heard it from me," Casey said, and he gave me a huge wink.

I went to the clubhouse to shower and change. All of a sudden, Mickey Mantle grabbed me by the arm and said, "Hey, Davey baby, Billy and a bunch of us are going out for a beer and something to eat. Come with us. And bring your girl if you like. We'll behave!"

"I'd love to," I said, trying to keep my cool. But inside I was thinking, *Wow—Mickey Mantle, Billy Martin and the guys want to have a beer with me. It's not a dream, but it sure is hard to believe!*

After all that, I needed to calm down, so I headed to the lounge for fifteen minutes of prayer and meditation.

Dear God, I silently prayed, *please keep me grounded and humble. Please look after me and help me be a good person. Thank You for the talent You've given me. I promise it won't be wasted or abused. I love You, I love You, I love You. And thank You for making it happen!*

A Happy Ending

After that, I was ready for anything. I took a hot shower and headed outside to meet Mom, Dad, Debbie and the fans.

Outside the stadium, there was a huge crowd waiting to get our autographs. I couldn't believe it—there must have been at least a thousand people there. We signed tons of autographs and posed for lots of pictures. The reporters were having a field day. I caught sight of Sandy in the crowd, who waved to me.

"You're famous, Dave!" she yelled. "Enjoy your big night!"

"Thanks!" I yelled back. "You're famous, too...enjoy yours!"

But there was really only three people I was looking for, and when I saw her red hat in the crowd, I felt better; that completed my day.

"Debbie!" I hollered over the voice of the crowd.

"Dave!" she yelled. Five seconds later, she was in my arms. We were both crying.

"I love you, Debbie," I whispered in her ear.

"I love you, too, Dave," she whispered back. "You're a star."

Mom and Dad were standing right behind Debbie.

"Duv, you've come a long way. We're so proud of you," my Dad said, with one hand firmly grasping my shoulder. He then said, "I love you very much." My Mom stood by and smiled sweetly, speechless with tears in her eyes, and said to my Dad, "Morris, our son, THE BALLPLAYER." Dad proudly said, "Yes, Claire, our son, THE BALLPLAYER!".

I knew I made mistakes in the past, but in this one moment, I felt they had all been reconciled. The commotion around us began to get to me, and I couldn't remember if I felt this way ever before in my life.

It's not a dream, I told myself. It's not a dream...

But, then, it was. It was a dream, in its own way. A real one, a living dream—one that I hoped would go on forever.

And for the first moment since I quit my role as warlord, I knew I was finally out.

Maybe I'll have a long career with the Yankees, or maybe this one start was a fluke. Who knows. But I'll walk the talk and give it my best shot. I'll never forget Irena who will always be in my thoughts and prayers.

But one thing was sure, I was free.

And now Debbie and I were going out to have a couple of beers... with Mickey Mantle and Billy Martin.

Who said there wasn't a God?

The Legend Begins

A Happy Ending

OFFICERS
PRESIDENT . . . . . . FRED HANEY
1ST VICE-PRES. . . . . JOE DIMAGGIO
2ND VICE-PRES. . . . WALTER ALSTON
3RD VICE-PRES. . , HOLLIS THURSTON
SEC.-TREAS.
CHARLES "CHUCK" STEVENS

930 E. WARDLOW RD. - SUITE #4
LONG BEACH, CALIFORNIA 90807
PHONE: (213) 424-7849

ASSOCIATION OF PROFESSIONAL BALL PLAYERS OF AMERICA

DIRECTORS
JOE CRONIN
AL LOPEZ   ALVIN DARK
MICKEY MANTLE   DON DRYSDALE
                WILLIE MAYS
BOB FELLER   CASEY STENGEL
GIL HODGES   TED WILLIAMS

ADVISORY COUNCIL
CALVIN R. GRIFFITH   PAUL RICHARDS
ANDREW A. HIGH C.C. JOHNSON SPINK
JOHN J. MCHALE   EDDIE SAWYER

March 8, 1972

Dear Dave:

I am very pleased to welcome you as a Life Member, and enclose your Life Card No. 2515.

For your years of interest and participation in the affairs of our Association, I thank you.

Kindest regards, and all good wishes.

Cordially,

"Chuck" Stevens
Secretary-Treasurer

CAS/jm

encl.

The letter above was received by David Oliphant on March 8, 1972. Please note, the historic Baseball Hall of Fame names under Officers, Directors and Advisory Council.